Barby Leathers
November 2007

Nancy Crampton

Aimee Phan was born in 1977 in Orange County, California, and now teaches creative writing at Washington State University, where she is at work on a novel. Visit her Web site at www.aimeephan.com.

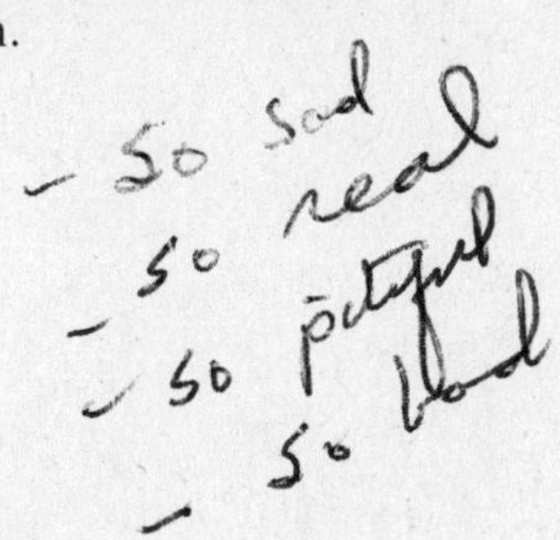

AIMEE PHAN

We Should Never Meet

STORIES

Picador
St. Martin's Press
New York

Though the stories are inspired by historical events, this is a work of fiction. All names, characters, places, and incidents either are the product of the author's imagination or are used fictitiously, and any resemblance to actual persons, living or dead, events, or locales is entirely coincidental.

 For information, address Picador, 175 Fifth Avenue, New York, N.Y. 10010.

www.picadorusa.com

Picador® is a U.S. registered trademark and is used by St. Martin's Press under license from Pan Books Limited.

For information on Picador Reading Group Guides, as well as ordering, please contact Picador.
Phone: 646-307-5626
Fax: 212-253-9627
E-mail: readinggroupguides@picadorusa.com

Some of the stories in this collection have appeared elsewhere in slightly different form: "Miss Lien" in *Prairie Schooner,* "We Should Never Meet" in *Colorado Review,* "The Delta" in *Michigan Quarterly Review,* "Visitors" in *Chelsea,* "Gates of Saigon" in *Virginia Quarterly,* and "Motherland" in *Meridian.*

Library of Congress Cataloging-in-Publication Data

Phan, Aimee.
We should never meet : stories / Aimee Phan.
p. cm.
Contents: Miss Lien—We should never meet—The delta—Visitors—Gates of Saigon—Emancipation—Bound—Motherland.
ISBN 0-312-32267-4
EAN 978-0-312-32267-0
1. Ho Chi Minh City (Vietnam)—Fiction. 2. Orange County (Calif.)—Fiction. 3. Vietnamese Americans—Fiction. 4. Refugees—Fiction. 5. Adoptees—Fiction. 6. Orphans—Fiction. I. Title.

PS3616.H36W4 2004
813'.6—dc22 2004051295

First published in the United States by St. Martin's Press

10 9 8 7 6 5 4 3 2

For my family and Matt

CONTENTS

We

Should

Never

Meet

MISS LIEN

LIEN WAS FIGHTING THEM again. Clawing at their arms, kicking her feet, pushing them away.

Go get the boy. This one is strong.

She rolled her head from one side to the other. Her skin was slick, sweat squeezing from every pore in her body, but there were still so many hands holding her down. Lien tried to focus on the ceiling. She knew it was dark cement, she remembered that from several hours earlier, but all she saw were bright blues and purples, growing lighter and lighter.

Push. Push now.

She tried to do what they said, she knew it would make the pain stop. But they still weren't satisfied. They kept wanting her to push harder. They were beginning to sound angry.

We need more sheets. It's getting slippery.

Why is all this blood coming from such a small girl?

That's probably why. Her body is still so young. It isn't prepared for this.

Little slut. All right. Let's try this again.

Push. Push now.

Their voices were getting fainter. Lien tried to lift her head up to hear them better, but a rough hand pushed it back onto the mat. Another gripped at her hair, pulling her head even farther back, ripping several strands from her damp scalp.

Push. Push.

Now all she could see were the colors. She wanted to tell them she was trying. She really was. But the only thing they could hear were her soft, shallow breaths, quieter and quieter.

The silt below Lien's feet was soft. Silky. She felt her heels, then the soles and toes sink into the soil until finally she looked down to see that the earth had swallowed her up to her ankles. Lien twisted playfully, testing her balance. The earth's grip on her was tight, secure.

Her brothers' voices rang far away. They were playing beyond their family's rice paddy, near the main road where the ground was solid enough to run on. It would take them a while to grow bored enough to come bother her. By then, her parents would be home from the market, and she and her sisters would help their mother and grandmother prepare dinner. But for now, she was alone. A slight breeze rustled the still water and cooled the sweat pooling on the back of her neck. She closed her eyes, enjoying it. The oldest of seven children, Lien was hardly ever alone.

The July monsoon season had ended, and for the first time in weeks the sky was clear, and the sun soared high, brightening the rich green of the fields and thick shade trees. Soon they would be planting rice seedlings for a new crop. While her family's plot of land was not nearly as vast as the rich plantations farther north in the Mekong Delta, it was adequate enough to feed Lien, her grandparents, parents, and younger siblings.

She looked to the earth. Her shadow stretched across the field, long and looming, intimidating. Since she could remember, Lien had always been impatient to grow, wanted to be as imposing as her father and grandfather. She imagined that with each passing year, she would grow taller and taller until she was as lofty as the trees and could step into heaven and be with her other grandparents, her mother's parents, the ones who died before she was born. When she confided this plan to her parents—she must have been only four or so—they'd laughed.

And what will you say to them, Miss Lien? her mother asked, using the family's favorite endearment for their oldest child.

I will say I am your granddaughter. I am your family. Love me.

The air was getting thick again. Lien couldn't breathe.

Mother. Turning slightly, Lien's spine curled to the cramping in her stomach.

Mother. A cool, callused hand brushed her forehead, and Lien lifted her neck instinctively to the touch. But then the hand went away and was soon replaced with fresh beads of sweat.

The fever is gone. Rest more.

Mother, wait. It was all Lien could manage. Her mouth was dry. It hurt to swallow.

Go to sleep.

The voice was harder this time, full of annoyance and authority. So she did.

Nearly twelve years old, their water buffalo could still plow fourteen-hour days, as familiar with the paddy as Lien. The rides happened after the day's work, when the air was cooling and Lien's father was sure their grandparents weren't around to see. They wouldn't approve of wasting the animal's precious energy, which should be reserved solely for plowing the fields.

Lien sat in the front, while her two younger sisters, Hanh and Doanh, clutched her waist from behind. The buffalo moved steadily through the swampy ditches, but the children still shrieked with elated terror, a gratifying scream after so many hours spent quietly hunched over a muddy field, poking fussy rice seeds into the water, one by one.

Up high, Lien observed her family's land. Her youngest brothers and sisters played with the pigs and ducks in the wire pen next to the house, chasing them, imitating their screeching and flapping. Her mother and grandmother squatted in the garden, pulling up ripened vegetables. Her mother rolled back on her heels, trying to keep a delicate balance over her swollen stomach.

Grasping the buffalo's thick black hide, Lien remembered the night her mother announced her most recent pregnancy. The adults' reaction had been different from previous ones. There were no smiles or shouts of good fortune. Her father's face had turned red, though he said nothing in front of the children. Her grandparents spent most of the night praying to their ancestors. This confused Lien, who'd always been told that every child was a blessing, an extra pair of hands and feet to enrich and strengthen the family.

They are worried about my health because I'm getting older,

Lien's mother had said when they were in the kitchen scrubbing potatoes. Certainly they will love this child, too.

We want this baby, don't we?

Of course. Silly girl. Every child born in our family is wanted.

Her mother was right. After several days, her grandparents and father were smiling and speaking of the baby with anticipation. But Lien knew it wasn't her mother's age that worried them.

Beyond the hills, the sky was smoking, but not with the soft pinks and oranges Lien had grown up watching every evening. The fiery shades were pointed and harsh. Cinders lingered in the air.

What is that smell? her sister Hanh asked.

They must be burning crop stubble, their father said.

Lien said nothing, and neither did her sisters. They clung closer to her waist. The buffalo shifted his weight restlessly.

The war is far away, their father assured them, far up in the north. We are safe here.

Because he was their father, because they never remembered him ever being wrong, they tried to believe him.

This time, Lien remembered where she was. She didn't have to open her eyes. Though the river breeze drifting in from the window was cool, biting even, the thin blanket clung to her back, already soaked with sweat. Long strands of hair pasted to her cheeks. The pungent aroma of peppermint oil tingled her nose. Lying on the sleeping mat these past two days, she recognized every sound the midwife and her servants made. Shuffling feet kicking up dust from the dirty floor. The steady drip of sheets and rags wrung clean. Jugs of water splashing into shallow clay bowls. The persistent, steady chorus of moaning and whimpering from the other girls. Lien vainly remained silent, hoping the others would recognize the dignity in swallowing back the pain. Hoping they would follow her example. But they didn't care. Their bodies, so recently torn open, were still in shock and ached, bled, and throbbed, resentful of what they'd been put through.

The midwife was making her rounds, checking temperatures and bandages while chewing on betel nuts. Lien sat up when she came near. Sparks of colors swirled around her eyes. She tightened her grip on the blanket to steady herself.

When can I leave?

The midwife placed her palm on Lien's forehead. What about the child?

Lien blinked several times and inhaled stale air. When can we leave?

The midwife spread her lips, revealing black-lacquered teeth. Lien realized she must have come from a family of wealth. Lien wondered how the woman had fallen from her upper status. The war, probably. It explained her bitterness. She disdained this place as well, thought she didn't belong here either.

You haven't paid me yet, the woman said.

Lien had been in and out of consciousness for the past two days. She knew the little money she did have, stuffed deep in the stitching of her clothes, was gone by now.

I will pay you back.

You had a difficult labor. We had to send for a boy to help hold you down.

I have nothing to offer you now, unless you want me to work the payment off. Around them, girls shuffled about the house, changing bedsheets, sweeping the dirt floor, tending to others either recovering or approaching labor. The midwife had enough people working off debts.

The midwife's eyes were distracted by something. Lien followed the woman's gaze to her wrist. A thin jade bracelet, her last possession of value. Without hesitating, Lien wrapped her fingers and wrenched it off, ignoring the dull pain it left behind.

I will be back for it when I have your money.

You can stay one more day, the midwife said, taking the bracelet from her and slipping it inside her blouse pocket. The bleeding should stop by tomorrow.

It is only a safety precaution. It is nothing to worry about. We can always use more room in this house with the new baby.

These were the things Lien's father kept saying while he, her mother, and grandparents began digging for a bunker behind their house. Almost every family in the village was building one. A ditch dug up for every house. Children started standing closer to their parents, holding on to their legs. The shelling, once barely audible in their village, was increasing in volume and frequency. The earth shook from these mounting explosions, unstable, uncertain, rattling the people who depended on its rich soil for their livelihood.

At first their father insisted the children concentrate on rice planting while the adults tended to the bunker. He said the rice was more important, the foundation of their family and the entire country. They depended on the crop for survival. Nothing should ever come before it or compromise its growth.

It promised to be an abundant crop. The monsoon season had provided plenty of water, and the mud's consistency was especially soupy this year. If successful, they would have enough rice left over to sell to the market for extra food and supplies to stock up for the dry season.

Though Lien sternly instructed her brothers and sisters to watch the paddy, she couldn't help also feeling curious about the adults' new project. She found herself walking along the edge of the paddy close to where they were digging and setting up plates of cement for the bunker walls. She prodded the buffalo absentmindedly with her bamboo stick as it plowed the field, all the while watching her father and grandfather fit the poles along the walls. She could only see the tops of their heads, light with dust and bent close together, like they were deep in conversation.

Perhaps we should send the women and children away, Lien's grandfather said. In the bunker's trench, they couldn't even see Lien.

Where would we send them? her father said. We don't know anyone in Can Tho.

They should go to the city. It's better protected. They will be safer there.

We have no money. We can't afford to. And we can't leave the land unguarded.

What good is this land going to do you if your family is dead?

Crazy old man. Has the village been attacked yet? I only agreed to build this bunker because you wouldn't stop nagging. No one is going to die. You heard Dat, it will never get this far south.

I am crazy? All my life this country has been at war, on my very land. How did I raise a son so blind?

The buffalo snorted loudly, restless from standing still for so long. Lien's father and grandfather looked up, squinting at the sun.

What are you doing, Miss Lien? her father asked. What do you need?

Nothing. The buffalo is just tired. She slapped the ox on the back with her stick, and they walked on.

The common room in the midwife's house was divided into five sections with bamboo screens for every two sleeping mats. The girl sharing Lien's partition, who'd given birth yesterday and slept most of the afternoon away, awoke just when the sun was setting, soft yellow light drifting over as her eyes fluttered open. A slow smile appeared on her face, her arms lazily stretching over her head. She was beautiful, with shiny waist-long black hair and delicate slender hands.

I'm starving. She sat up a little and looked over at Lien. When is supper?

Soon.

Ay-yah. The girl lay back suddenly, but her smile only grew wider. You think it would get easier after a few times, but it never does. Her eyes scanned Lien head to toe. Your first?

Lien nodded.

Oh, look at this one. One of the midwife's servants was walking toward them holding a small bundle wrapped in cloth. The girl held her arms out for it, quickly cradling and cooing at it softly. This will be a handsome one. Daddy's an American GI. Beautiful green eyes. But it's too soon to tell if it will get those.

Do you want to see your baby?

It took Lien several moments to realize the midwife's servant was talking to her. Even then Lien couldn't speak, only staring back at the servant's expectant eyes, then the girl's.

Both were waiting for Lien's response, ready to judge her. Finally, reluctantly, Lien nodded.

The girl had pulled her blouse down to breast-feed the infant. Lien turned on her back so she could stare at the ceiling.

It's all right, the girl said after the servant left. I wasn't sure about looking at my first either, knowing I had to give it up.

Lien rolled her head to the side and looked at her. Where did you take it?

There's this orphanage run by some Catholic nuns. The girl shifted the infant so she could sit up more easily. They take every child in, no questions.

How far is that from here?

Just outside of Vinh Long. About fifteen kilometers north. The girl smiled sympathetically. You know, this baby could help you, if the father's an American. That's why I'm keeping this one.

Lien didn't say anything.

Unless you don't want to see the father. Once again the girl's eyes traveled the length of Lien's face and body, as if she could tell just by looking at her. Unless it was bad. Then no one could blame you for getting rid of it.

Lien twisted in her sheets until she found a comfortable position facing the wall. I can't keep it.

They were silent then, the only sound in the room the persistent, greedy suckling of the infant. Lien resisted the urge to cover her ears, though the nursing only grew louder and more desperate.

They had to be quiet. The roof of the bunker was made up of thin layers of straw and sand. Lien held her brother An in her lap, urging him to stop wiggling and hushing his crying. No one spoke. The family spent most of the time listening to the fighting and burning above, trying not to envision the worst.

When it had been silent for nearly five hours, and her father deemed it safe, they emerged from the bunker with tentative steps, squinting, like it had been years since they'd seen the sun and breathed fresh air, instead of only two days.

We're alive, Lien's mother reminded them. We need to be thankful we are alive.

But as the family wandered around their property to assess the damage, they could not remember that. It didn't matter that the house was spared.

Most of the livestock had been stolen from their cages. The vegetable garden was covered in shrapnel. They found their water buffalo near the main road slaughtered, rotting, covered with flies. But the worst of it was the rice paddy. The crop was ruined. The smell of fire drifted through the air. They'd have no rice for the coming season.

Lien was the only one to follow her father into the rice paddy. He walked through each ditch, as if to confirm that every seedling had been uprooted, destroyed. Lien kept up as best she could, but the burnt rice stalks sliced deep into her bare feet, slowing her down. When she caught up to him near the edge of their property, he was staring at the ground. He sank his knees into the crusty, dry dirt and dug into the earth with both hands. He held it up to Lien. All their work, all those hours, weeks, and years. Now ash and gunpowder.

We can replant, Lien said. We can try again.

Her father shook his head. It's too late. We'll have to wait for next season.

But what are we going to eat? She could feel it creeping into her voice. She swallowed hard, wanting to will the fear away.

Since she was little, Lien had always been grateful to be born into her family. Unlike others in the village, their family valued daughters as highly as sons. Each child considered special and necessary. They looked down on other families who spoiled their sons and ignored their daughters, thought them to be old-fashioned, outdated, cruel.

Lien had always been treated like a firstborn son, with all the privileges and honors. Now she suddenly understood the responsibility that came with those benefits and, for the first time, wished she were a boy. Sons could go out and make money in place of the father and support the family. Daughters didn't have the same liberties.

The servant returned with it. Tiny. Wrinkly. Slippery. Smelling like sour milk and feces. Its eyes hadn't opened yet. Lien held it away from her, tilting and inspecting it like her fish at the market.

The baby looks strong, the girl said. It looks like you.

No it doesn't.

The servant said the infant had already been fed. Lien wordlessly handed it back to her.

Every patient's possessions lay beside her mat against the wall. On the girl's side were several bags neatly stuffed with clothes and toiletries. There was nothing on Lien's side. Lien was used to the look the girl gave her now: compassion, pity, a little smugness. She tried to ignore it.

You know, if you need money, the girl said, I know some people—

I already have a job.

What do you do?

I work on a fishing boat in Can Tho.

But you know you can make a lot more—

I'm not a whore. Lien didn't mean to sound rude. But she was tired. The walls were beginning to bend and wobble again.

The girl didn't seem to take offense. She even smiled. I wasn't either. And I won't be for much longer. But it's nice to eat. It's nice to provide for your family.

Later that evening, a servant arrived with their suppers. Rice porridge with chicken shreds. Lien savored every bite, even swallowing her pride to ask for another bowl. Part of her regretted that she'd be leaving tomorrow. She hadn't eaten this well since she was home. But she would be home soon.

She should have left immediately. Instead, waiting a week only served to divide the family even more. Lien's grandparents did not approve of her leaving for the city alone. Her parents felt there was no other choice. There was no money, and their food supplies were dwindling. Lien's father couldn't leave his young family and land unprotected. Her mother was expecting the baby in a few weeks. Lien's grandparents were too old. Her brothers and sisters were too young. Lien would go to Can Tho, the largest city in the Delta, to find work in the floating market. She would send money home and return after the next monsoon season in time for replanting the rice.

The night before she left, their family cooked a small chicken and the last of the wild sweet potatoes, giving the largest portion to Lien so she would have strength for her journey. Her brothers and sisters took turns sitting next to her while they ate, mostly in silence. She rubbed each of them roughly behind their ears, instructing them to be good for their parents.

Her grandfather reminded Lien of their country's long history of oppression and survival: first the Chinese, then the French, the Japanese, now each other. He'd been imprisoned and released from three regimes because it was his fate to survive. You will too, Miss Lien. You will because you are strong like me.

Her grandmother gave her several gold-plated necklaces and a jade bracelet, which she'd been saving as part of Lien's dowry. Her hands were cold when she held Lien's cheeks. Remember you are a good girl. Stay away from bad people. Do not do anything to shame us.

Her father dressed her in his warmest coat. Look how tall you are getting. Almost as tall as me. Your father is getting old now. He is not as smart as he once was. But you are, more than I ever was. You are my hope.

Her mother's eyes were wet, but she put on a bright smile for her daughter. She brushed Lien's long black hair and tied it into a knot on the top of her head. You should keep your hair up so people will know you come from a good family. I won't be able to do it for you anymore. You have to. You're an adult now.

Take care of yourself.

We are so proud of you.

Come home safe.

Do not let us down.

Lien leaned over and saw her reflection, exaggerated and ugly, bleeding into dirty water and lily pads, frowning back. At least eight meters.

There was no other way to cross the canal but to use the monkey bridge. The child's weight bore heavily in Lien's arms, though it couldn't have been more than six, seven pounds. Alone, she'd prance across the creaky bridge, vine-stitched skeins of mangrove and bamboo, without another thought. She'd done it so many times before. But now this extra weight on her hip. This unfamiliar caution. It compromised her balance. It made her weak.

She'd left the midwife's house that morning. Lien had to wrap up the infant in old newspaper since they needed the blanket for other babies. She hadn't been walking for that long, but her back and feet already throbbed. Someone at the midwife's house had stolen her conical hat, and though she tried to stay under the shade of trees, there was no escaping the humidity. She had to stop frequently to breathe properly. Her hair stuck to her forehead and temples, the sweat dripping down and stinging her eyes. It wouldn't be that much farther. She would reach the orphanage before sunset.

Right foot on the bamboo. Don't look down. Left foot. Careful of the loose bamboo. Hold the infant closer. Closer. Hold it near the center of the chest or you'll tip over. Right. Left. Again. Again. Keep the weight on the balls of the feet. Light steps, light steps. Stay moving. Right. Left. Ignore the baby. Keep on moving. It's awake. It's squirming. Stop squirming. Right. Left.

Halfway across, the baby started to cry, and without meaning to, Lien looked down to the water. Her balance shifted, and she felt the weight pull at her from the side. Instinctively, she swung the other way, trying to right herself. She pressed the infant's head with her left hand into her chest, muffling its cries. A flutter in her stomach, the realization that she could fall threw her forward, running across the bridge until she finally reached the other side, falling onto the dirt road, gasping until she could breathe again.

The infant bawled. Its wrinkly face screwed up in pain, infuriated that it was startled. The infant had been so good thus far, so quiet. Now its screams were all she could hear.

It's okay, she said, patting the infant on the back, it's okay. She pulled the infant away and looked into its face, its eyes folded slits, face bloodred, mouth a tiny oval, wailing. It looked no different from any one of Lien's younger brothers or sisters when they were born. Pure, blameless. She reached for the newspaper cradling its head, pulling it over to cover its face. It didn't stop the crying, but Lien felt better.

Hey little thing.

Lien looked up, squinting beneath her conical hat, at the blond-haired GI hovering above her, his large hairy hands on his hips. He stood at the edge of the dock. Lien crouched on the fishing sampan, safe with a foot of green water between them.

Wanna buy? Lien asked. She knew only a few phrases of English, enough to haggle against experienced bargainers for the fish she sold. Number one fish. Very good.

Not the fish, honey.

Cai Rang was the largest floating market in Can Tho and all of the Mekong Delta. Lien awoke before dawn, gutting, cleaning, and selling fish until sundown in exchange for food, lodging, and a small share of money. The fishermen, two brothers who looked as old as her father but with no families of their own, seemed kind enough, but she felt uncomfortable sleeping in the same cabin with them. Lien talked of her father often, how large and angry he was and how he would be visiting Can Tho soon.

Still, they'd stroke her hair, squeeze her hip. She felt compelled to allow this. It had taken her several weeks wandering Can Tho to find this job, and she couldn't lose it.

The city was different from what she remembered. The floating market was still the center of trade, where boats and sampans gathered to sell their fish, vegetables, and fruit. Her grandmother had taken her here several times to barter their rice. Lien remembered it to be friendlier than it was now. Maybe it was because she was younger then.

But the people did seem colder, more distant, perhaps because of the Americans. Soldiers, taller than she ever imagined people could be, were everywhere. It made the merchants nervous. Many of the soldiers stared at Lien curiously when she would yell to them, waving catfish in their faces. Some even tried to talk to her, like this one.

C'mon. You want to get some lunch with me, little thing?

Lien tilted her head to the side and smiled softly at the GI. No speak good. Sorry. You buy fish or no?

He stepped toward her, one heavy black boot landing on the sampan. Surprised, Lien fell backwards, her hands desperately reaching behind to clutch the soggy wood floor. A large, curly-haired hand reached for her shoulder.

C'mon, honey. You don't have to be scared of me.

A crate of fish dropped on the floor, rocking the sampan. Both Lien and the GI turned to see one of the fishermen, the older of the two brothers, approach them. The GI's hand released Lien, and he retreated to the dock. Smiling sheepishly, he offered a mock salute before turning to leave.

The older brother knelt at the edge of the boat, scowling at Lien. You better stop flirting with those white soldiers.

I wasn't flirting.

Don't lie to me. He strode toward her, his face a deep red in the bright sun. I won't tolerate whores or liars on my boat.

She flinched when he raised his hand toward her, but it was a caress that came and not a strike. Along her cheek and down her neck, fingering a strand of hair from her bun that swept past her shoulder.

Stay away from those men. His eyes were soft now, his mouth relaxing into a disapproving frown. We've lost too many of our girls to them.

Lien nodded, trying to hide her relief when he took his hand away. He stared at her for a long time before he gathered his fishing nets and returned to the back of the boat.

At nights, she would remember her family, and this allowed her eventually to drift into sleep. The money she earned would go to them, and, once there was enough, she would leave to help for the next rice planting. But after the February monsoon season, her father sent her a letter asking if she could stay in Can Tho for a bit longer. The money was too valuable. So Lien stayed. This was her responsibility.

It wouldn't stop crying. They were resting in a cool spot under a papaya tree, a little off the main road where beggars and American soldiers couldn't hassle her. Her bare feet were bleeding again. She dug them into the moist soil to cool them off. She shook the child softly, trying to coax it back to sleep; but it would have none of that, howling with lungs that Lien had to admit were impressive. Lien was hungry. She hadn't had lunch. That was when she realized it hadn't eaten since that morning either.

Gingerly, she lifted her blouse to expose her left breast. Holding the hem of her blouse up with her teeth, she tucked the infant's head to her breast until its quivering mouth latched on to her nipple. Its grip was tight, painful, and she nearly pulled the infant away. But the screaming stopped. The infant's face relaxed, finally getting what it wanted. She held it there for what seemed like hours until it was sated. But even then Lien couldn't get up to start walking again right away. She was drained and, unlike the infant, had no food readily available.

Lien stumbled along the market street, her arms crossed around her midsection, trying to contain the pain.

It's too strong, the herbalist had told her, it won't die.

She walked as quickly as she could, but people kept getting in her way. Shoulders bumping into her. She swerved to avoid a cyclo taxi backing out of an alley and slipped on the loose gravel, landing hard on her side. Her right hand was scraped from the fall, bleeding. Someone tried to help her up, but she pushed him away. Lien couldn't stand to be touched anymore. She took a few steps, trying to regain her balance and direction. Faces all around stared at her. Lien wanted to yell at them to leave her alone. She never meant for this to happen.

Because it wouldn't die, it had gotten angry at the herbs Lien ingested, retaliating with more nausea, more cramps. Five months. She had five months until it was out of her body. She needed to work as much as she could until then.

Finally, she regained her sense of direction. She walked in silence, jealously taking in all the yelling and noise around her. They had the freedom, the luxury to speak, complain, cry, and release. Lien could tell no one of this. She could never confide to her mother and father. It wouldn't make anything better.

Silly and childish to think it would. They would only blame her. They would never believe that they were partly responsible. No, Lien would take care of this on her own. She survived this long in the city by herself. She could handle it.

A long dirt driveway led to a tall rusted gate surrounded by an equally large concrete wall. Blessed Haven for the Children of God. Lien pushed the broken gate open and walked up the driveway to a two-story building with peeling paint and covered with vines. She could already hear the crying from inside, seeping through the cracks of the walls.

Lien had been crouching in the bushes outside the driveway for several hours until the nuns had closed the windows after sunset. From what she could see, it seemed like an adequate place. It would be well taken care of here.

She cautiously walked up the driveway, ready to retreat should someone open the front door. Once there, she carefully laid the infant on the front step. It squirmed, and, for a brief moment, Lien feared would scream again. But its mouth only opened to yawn, and it settled back into sleep.

Lien pulled at the bell hard. She turned and ran, suddenly overcome with an energy that had been sorely missed all day. Each step felt so light the wind was almost carrying her until she passed the gate and turned, hiding behind the wall.

Someone had opened the front door. A nun wearing a black habit stepped out, looking down at the bundle on the front step. She peered beyond the gate, but Lien remained out of sight. Lien waited.

The nun simply stood there, looking out, hands on her hips, waiting. Could she see Lien? It was impossible. What was she looking for? Lien crouched lower, breathing heavily through her mouth. The girl said this orphanage took all babies, no questions. What was she doing? They couldn't refuse the child. They were nuns. Did they need the mother's approval? Did they need Lien to say she couldn't keep this child, that there was no possible way she could ever care for it?

It wasn't fair. So many open mouths and outstretched hands, expecting her to fill them. She couldn't have another one. She didn't ask for this.

Finally, the nun bent over and picked up the infant. One final look out on the road, one last chance, and she turned her back and stepped in. Lien rested her head against the cool cement wall. This child was safe. This child would not have to suffer. The door shut behind the nun. Lien watched for several minutes, waiting, resting, breathing, then turned and began for the main road.

WE

SHOULD

NEVER

MEET

IT WAS VULNERABLE. HIDDEN in the corner of an old strip mall several blocks from Magnolia, the edge of Little Saigon. Hardly any cops at this hour. The store's owner must have been stupid to pick this location. Like Vinh said, you can't have sympathy for everyone, especially stupid people.

Kim wasn't planning on doing anything awful. She wasn't like that. Sure, she had been asked by old classmates and some of Vinh's friends to join in on jobs. Her height was an asset; so was the ambiguity of her racial makeup. Lots of people mistook her for Hispanic, sometimes even white. But Kim wasn't interested. She'd seen what it did to Vinh. She wasn't like that. There were better ways to make cash. She worked at the Tasty Burger near her old foster home and made enough not to have to take those kinds of risks.

But this was an emergency. She'd accidentally smashed Vinh's beeper the night before and needed to replace it before he found out. Fifty-five dollars he had to go and spend on some flashy silver-tinted one, the most expensive on the market. Vain Vinh, Vain Vinh. The store's pager display was behind the register, but close to the exit. Kim needed a twenty-second distraction.

Forget it, Mai had told her earlier that morning.

You don't have to do anything. You only have to talk to her.

I'm not helping you steal. Can't I just lend you the money?

For a beeper? No way. Kim hated beepers. The idea of being reached anytime, anywhere didn't have the same appeal to her as it did to her ex-boyfriend.

If you hate them so much, why are you borrowing Vinh's?

He made me.

He made you, Mai said, narrowing her eyes. Then why should you care if he knew you broke it?

Because Kim didn't want to owe Vinh anything else. She was already staying at his apartment, a tiny two-bedroom in Santa Ana that he shared with three other friends—*temporarily*—until she could afford a place of her own. It was bad enough letting Vinh think there was a chance they would get back together. She didn't need this too.

C'mon Mai, Kim said. You're the only one who can help me.

It was true. Kim's other foster sisters looked too dirty. Always getting followed in department stores for their grimy jeans and dark lip liner. Mai had a sweet, clean face. And the clueless way she shuffled around, always bumping into things. It could not be faked.

It didn't take much more for Kim to convince Mai. It never did. Kim had known Mai since they were kids. They'd been placed in several foster homes together, along with Vinh. Though not blood-related, Mai always obeyed Kim, like a younger sister should.

They were supposed to meet outside the store at three. It was already a quarter after, and Kim felt antsy just standing around. Made her look suspicious. The afternoon sun was still high, giving the store's sign, MEKONG GIFTS AND COLLECTIBLES, a blinding glare when looked at directly.

This was a particularly depressing strip mall. A cheaply built two-story building painted a bland cream and streaked gray from pollution. It housed some of the typical Little Saigon businesses: hair salon, chiropractor's office, bakery, and minimart. The bare parking lot was sparsely populated with thin, newly transplanted trees, wilting in their blacktop surroundings.

Kim lifted her long hair away from her sweaty neck. It was too hot. The sidewalk felt bumpy under her sneakers from the black gum stains covering the concrete. The smell of rotten Coke wafting from the nearby minimart was making her nauseous. Mai wouldn't change her mind. She would never stand Kim up.

A small figure in a yellow tank top and jeans slunk from around the corner of the shopping center. Kim smiled. Mai, so loyal and good. Still those long minutes waiting for her reminded Kim that it wouldn't always be this way. Mai was growing up. She would graduate from high school this year. Probably go on to college. She wouldn't mean to, but she'd leave Kim behind.

I hate this, Mai said once she stood in front of Kim. She shifted her backpack to her other shoulder. Can I say how much I hate this?

Later, Kim said, pushing her friend toward the store.

Mai glared at her before walking to the door and stepping in. Kim watched through the glass window as Mai made her way to the register to talk with the middle-aged Vietnamese woman behind the counter. After a few minutes, the woman nodded and stepped out from behind the counter to show Mai the fabrics hanging from the far wall.

Kim pushed open the glass door, dangling chimes from the hinge signaling her arrival. The storekeeper didn't even turn to look. Kim let the door slip shut behind her. Perfect.

What size dress does your mother wear? the woman asked Mai in Vietnamese. They studied the rich emerald greens and brilliant canary yellows used for traditional Vietnamese gowns.

I don't know, Mai said. She's not much bigger than me. Her voice was shaky, tipping with guilt. Kim silently willed her to calm down.

There weren't any cameras in the store. No detectors along the doors. Small gift shops like these never had them, making them such convenient targets. Like the others, it had more merchandise than shelf space, with porcelain and glass items stacked on top of each other, dangerously close to toppling over and shattering on the linoleum floor.

Behind the counter, Vinh's beeper hung two rows in from the left. When she was sure the woman was fully preoccupied, Kim took one step behind the counter and carefully lifted the package from its hook. Kim looked up. Their backs were still turned. Kim took a shallow breath and slipped the beeper behind her, tucking it into her underwear. When it slipped a little, Kim twisted around to pull it back in place.

What are you doing? a voice asked.

Kim lifted her head. Her hair fell over her eyes, but between the strands Kim saw the woman glaring at her, arms full of fabric. Beside her, Mai inched away.

Kim remained calm. She tilted her chin up at the woman, tossing her hair out of her eyes, trying to appear taller.

What is behind your back? the woman asked.

Kim turned to Mai and gave her a look. Go now.

Hey, the woman said when Mai stepped away and turned to rush out of the store. The woman looked back to Kim. What is this? Show me what you have.

Kim reached behind her and tossed the beeper on the counter.

The woman stared at the beeper, then at Kim. Kim stuffed her hands in her back jeans pockets, trying to appear relaxed, like Vinh would tell her to. She remembered the words. *Brookhurst 354,* Vinh's gang, her safety insurance. The storekeeper would think twice about calling the police once she knew Kim was under their protection.

Kim wondered why the woman hadn't said anything yet. She shifted her weight from one foot to another, her gaze still defiant. She would not apologize. She would admit nothing.

You should leave now, the woman finally said.

Kim nearly laughed out loud. What?

Leave, the woman said. There was a sternness in the woman's face, but also compassion—something new. Kim was used to insults and threats whenever she was caught stealing, especially when they recognized she was *my-lai.* But this woman only nodded at her, maybe even felt sorry for her because of her mixed race, and turned her back, expecting Kim to simply walk out, unpunished.

Mai stood waiting for her across the street, hidden behind a phone booth.

I didn't hear any screaming, Mai said. What happened?

Nothing, Kim said. She looked back at the store. Nothing happened.

Mai exhaled. You are so lucky. She looked like she was about to laugh, but she caught herself, her jaw retightened. You are never doing that again, she said.

No one was home when Kim returned to the apartment. The place seemed brighter, bigger when it was empty, which was hardly ever. She took a long shower, reheated some leftover Thai takeout she found in the back of the refrigerator, and sat down to watch some television.

Though the neighborhood was shit, wedged between a string of consignment shops and liquor stores, the apartment was pretty nice. The living room and bedrooms were a decent size, and while most of the furnishings were castoffs found on sidewalks and from garage sales, the entertainment system was excellent. Big-screen TV, 20-CD changer, two VCRs for dubbing, even a turntable. Kim had been doubtful when Vinh and the boys first lugged the system home, but for four months there had been no problems with anyone trying to break in and get it back.

Balancing chopsticks in one hand and the flipper in the other, Kim searched for something worthwhile on TV, staying no longer than a few seconds on each channel. She always judged her foster homes by the amount of television she was allowed. It gave a clue to how the next few months or years would be. A couple of hours, and the foster parents were strict assholes who wouldn't stop harassing her or ratting her out to the social worker. If no time limits were set, then they generally left her alone. Sometimes this was true. More often the dad was an asshole anyway and found other ways to bother her so that it wasn't freedom at all. And, of course, with Kim's luck those were the homes that took forever to get out of.

Here, there were no foster parents to tell her what to do. She could watch as much television as she wanted. She could go out whenever she wanted. Though he tried, Vinh couldn't control her. And he knew better than to try too hard.

Kim went to bed at eleven. Around two she heard them come home. The jangle of keys tossed on the kitchen table, the smell of cigarette smoke wafting through the thick SoCal heat. Kim wondered when Vinh would eventually get around to calling someone to fix the air conditioner. She didn't think she could last much longer like this. Hopefully she wouldn't, though, hopefully she'd be out of here by then. Kim turned her head into the pillow and pretended to be asleep.

The three boys shared one room while Kim and Vinh got the other. She heard the bedroom door creak open and shut. His jacket and jeans tossed off, probably left in a heap on the floor. Then his abrupt weight on the mattress, disturbing the bed's equilibrium. It was a twin, so Kim begrudgingly understood he had to touch her while they slept. He wiggled into place, his chest to her back, his right arm creeping around her stomach.

Kim clenched her teeth and kept her eyes shut. Since she could remember, Kim always slept on her side facing the wall. Vinh took that to mean she wanted to cuddle whenever they slept together.

I know you're not sleeping, Vinh said, his breath moist on her ear.

She turned on her back and pushed his arm off. Move over, it's too hot.

Don't you wanna know where I was? Vinh asked.

I know where you were.

No you don't, he said excitedly, brushing some hair away from Kim's face. His hands were sweaty. Kim wished that at least once, he'd go to the bathroom and wash up before coming to bed.

I was at a meeting with the Pomona Boys, he said.

It was too dark for Vinh to see Kim's true expression. Really.

Don't you get it, baby? he said, shaking her arm, like that would help. They could get us in with L.A., and then even Houston. Can you believe it?

Despite all Vinh's faults, he was ambitious, even if it was for stupid things, like furthering the prestige of Brookhurst 354, still considered a minor player by other gangs in Little Saigon. They'd only recently pulled off a string of successful home invasions.

What are you guys doing? Kim asked.

Couple of houses in Monterey Park. One of them has money in a pho chain up north. He and his family just moved out here.

Why do they need your help?

They're having problems losing the cops last few weeks.

So you guys can get caught.

She could feel Vinh pulling away from her, his enthusiasm deflating. Why do you have to say those things?

Kim turned to face him. Vinh wasn't bad-looking. She never would have been with him if he were. Even with his shaved head, he was still attractive, with his bright eyes and infectious smile. It was a shame he stood only an inch taller than she. Kim knew he couldn't help it, especially since she was so tall because of her white blood. But still, she held it against him. It always reminded her when she looked at him that he would never measure up. It was a terrible thing to think, but there it was.

Sorry, she said, not meaning it at all.

Why can't you be excited for us? Vinh asked. This is for you, too.

She didn't ask how because she didn't want to know. The alarm clock glowed a red 2:28, and Kim was tired.

Where were you tonight? Vinh asked. I tried paging you.

Did you? I didn't get it.

Maybe the battery's dead. He sat up. Where is it? I'll check.

It's in the living room. Do it tomorrow, okay? I'm tired. She pulled him toward her.

Vinh hesitated but finally relaxed and settled back into bed. He began tracing circles along her arms, slowly and softly, encouraging goose bumps, even though it was hot. Kim allowed this, hoping he'd eventually rub harder so it could be a real massage. But when he started pulling at her underwear, she stopped him.

What?

I don't want to.

What's wrong? More nightmares?

Yes.

Christ.

They were silent for a few minutes, but Kim could tell he was still awake and was going to try again.

Do you ever think about them? Kim asked.

Huh? He sounded sleepy. Maybe he didn't want sex.

Your parents. Where they are.

Christ, Vinh said. Have you been talking to Mai?

Shut up.

She does this every year, but not until the holidays. Why does she have to go getting you obsessed about it, too?

I am not obsessed. I was just wondering. Don't you ever wonder?

Not really.

Liar.

Why should I? We're twenty years old. We don't need them.

Don't you want to know if they're alive?

They're not, Vinh said. We're orphans.

You don't know that. Technically, Kim was classified as an orphan when she arrived in the States as part of Operation Babylift. But that didn't mean her parents were dead, only that they'd given her up. No identification on her but her name. Her real birthday was unknown. She was assigned the day January first along with every other orphan whose birth certificate was missing. Vinh's situation was similar, though he arrived later as an unaccompanied minor with the boat refugees. Neither had any idea if their parents were alive or not.

My parents are dead, Vinh said. It was a pronouncement he truly believed. He relaxed his arms around her, pulling the sheet up closer.

It didn't take long for his breathing to become heavier and steadier. Carefully, Kim extricated herself from his grip and crept closer to the wall, pulling her knees up toward her as much as she could, eventually falling asleep herself.

Usually Kim walked the direct route between the bus stop and work, but she found a detour, three blocks out of the way, to pass the gift shop where the woman had let her go. At first, Kim stayed on the opposite side of the street so the woman couldn't see her. Kim would slow down whenever she was within eyesight of the store and squint, trying to see if she was there.

Most of the time the woman sat at the counter behind the register, reading a magazine, talking on the phone, or helping one of the few customers that came in. After some observation, Kim guessed the woman was in her early forties. She remembered that the woman's accent sounded regionally southern and heavy, so she must have arrived in the States not too long ago.

Eventually Kim became braver, approaching the mall sidewalk, the parking lot, then the front of the store. But the woman didn't even look up, and Kim wondered if she'd forgotten her.

At work, Kim was taken off register duty after her manager caught her talking back to a customer. Nancy wasn't even there for the whole argument. If she had been, she would have understood why Kim refused to give the guy's kid a different play toy. Kid was a brat.

To learn her lesson that every child at Tasty Burger deserves a play toy, Kim was sentenced to sit in the kitchen during her shifts and assemble play meals. One cheap plastic toy in every paper box decorated with oversized crossword puzzles and knock-knock jokes.

Kim was at the register counter dropping off a box of assembled play meals when she saw the woman from the gift store. She headed for Frank's register where only three customers stood in line.

Hey, Kim said when Frank walked to the soda machine. Lemme take over your line.

I just took my fifteen, Frank said. Besides, you're not allowed yet.

Nancy's not here. C'mon, I'll take your Saturday shift.

Frank hesitated, but then nodded as he capped off his drinks. Frank was new—been there only a month—and hadn't earned a Saturday off yet.

The woman noticed when Kim smiled politely and asked to take her order. This was the closest they'd stood to each other since their first meeting. Kim memorized everything she could: long black hair in a simple ponytail that ran down her back, her face free of makeup so you could see the wrinkles around her eyes, sparse freckles on her cheeks, the mole on her chin.

You can come in, the woman said as Kim handed back her change. As long as you don't try to steal anything again.

After her shift, Kim was tempted just to pass the store and head home. She caught her reflection in a glossy bank window and was horrified. She looked terrible. Eight hours working had given her hat hair and she smelled like fries. She wanted to present a better picture of herself. The sun had started to melt into the freeway. Kim didn't like taking the bus after dark, but she knew she couldn't waste this opportunity.

The sign above the store flickered a bright neon green, the only place lit and still open on the strip mall. The woman sat once again behind the register. Kim walked in.

Keep your hands out, the woman said.

Kim slowly entered and looked around. There was no one else in the store. They stood across from each other, the counter between them.

Get much business? Kim asked.

It's been all right, the woman said. It isn't the best location, but it was all we could afford. A video store might open next door. That could help.

Anyone else helping you?

No. My husband has his own job.

What about your kids?

We don't have any children.

In the glass counter in front of Kim, jade bracelets and silver necklaces twinkled from the fluorescent lighting above.

Why did you say I could come in? Kim asked.

Why did you want to?

It sat there, lodged in Kim's throat, too afraid to be said, convinced it was too soon.

I don't know either, the woman said. But you seem harmless enough.

Kim's spine straightened. I am not harmless.

The woman smiled at her. You think you're so tough. All you young girls. It is considered disrespectful in Vietnam.

But not here.

No, she said, and that look, the so common mixture of relief and homesickness, trickled over the woman's face, deepening already existing worry lines around her mouth and eyes. Not here.

Kim's gaze retreated back to the jewelry, the jade bracelets, shades of green, red, white, and orange shining brilliantly in the black velvet background.

Do you see something you like? the woman asked.

Kim didn't respond, only glanced up to inspect the woman's own bracelet—green. Lots of Vietnamese women wore them. Tradition said the longer you wore the bracelet, the darker and more vivid the color became, indicating the wearer's maturity. It was a common gift between family members. Mai had gotten one from her foster mother for her sixteenth birthday.

How did you know I was Vietnamese? Kim asked. Hardly anyone could tell unless they were looking for it. But this woman knew right away, spoke to her in the native language the very first time.

Aren't you?

Yes.

I can tell, the woman said. The way you walk and carry yourself. It's obvious.

But I was raised here, Kim said, and, before she could stop herself, I'm an orphan.

The woman shook her head. It doesn't matter. Whoever raised you, wherever, you're Vietnamese.

Bells rang. Kim looked over her shoulder. Two older Vietnamese women sauntered in, engrossed in conversation, their slippers shuffling against the linoleum floor. The glass door shut, and the chimes tangled again.

Kim looked at her watch. The last bus to make her transfer left in five minutes.

I need to go, Kim said.

The woman looked slightly disappointed, but nodded. See you later.

Yeah, Kim said. Maybe. She walked out the door quickly, trying to ignore the bubbles in her chest, in anticipation for tomorrow, the next time they would meet.

It was Vinh's turn to host the meeting that night. She could hear them when she came up the stairs, their hard, relentless laughter, the vibrations of their heavy footsteps rippling throughout the building. Kim stood at the front door, taking it all in. There was no other way to enter the apartment.

Kimmy! a deep voice yelled. So many of them spread out in the living room like it was their home, their sticky hair gel and muddy sneakers smearing the carpet and couch, greasy pizza boxes and beer bottles tossed all over the floor and coffee table.

Hey, she said. She walked through the living room, stepping over various bodies, where several hands playfully grabbed for her ankles.

Where you been? asked Hung, one of Vinh's oldest friends, the one who'd gotten him into 354. We never see you anymore.

Gotta work, Kim said, tripping over someone's leg.

You make her work, Vinh? Kim, if you were with me, I'd make sure you never worry about cash.

The obvious laughter, leering. Kim was grateful when she reached the bedroom, shutting the door behind her, wishing it thick enough to keep all the noise out.

It wasn't so long ago she'd thought they were all so tough, fearless. She was grateful for their protection in high school, beating up assholes that harassed her. She listened intently to their tales of home invasions and robberies like a child at story time, cooed at their sleek Honda Civics and Integras with elaborate car kits and spoilers, and mistook their bad tempers for honor and pride. But that was high school. Some of the people in 354 were almost twenty-five, had no intentions of leaving to get a real job. They thought this was real. It embarrassed Kim to remember she once had, too.

While she changed out of her work clothes, Vinh walked in. He shut the door behind him and faced her. He looked drunk. Maybe a little stoned. Angry, too.

Why are you home so late?

Kim showed him her watch. It's eight-thirty.

You got off work today at five.

I was with Mai.

I called her.

Are you checking up on me?

Who are you seeing?

Kim sat on the bed. Vinh stepped closer until he was standing over her, like he was about to hit her, but she knew he wouldn't. You can't ask me that anymore, she said.

Why not? Vinh asked. His face though, she knew he knew. He was daring her to say it out loud. His eyes darted around the four walls, reminding her of what he had that she still needed.

Kim slid off the bed and away from him. I'm moving out.

At first he didn't say anything. He only twisted away, shoulders straight, inflated with pride. Right now? he asked.

No, Kim said. Next week.

I don't get you, Vinh said. What do you want from me?

Nothing. Kim looked to the floor, the stained, sooty carpet. She dug into her pocket and tossed his still-damaged beeper on the bed. You've done enough, thank you.

He wouldn't look at it.

I mean it, Kim said. Really. She hoped she sounded grateful, but it was such an unfamiliar sentiment, she wasn't sure how to do it.

Christ, Vinh said. I don't care.

Kim thought she'd feel relief. So many months of guilt and dread about leading him on, her first kiss, her only boyfriend, her oldest friend. Now he finally knew. But there was no peace, no release from her chest or pressure lifted from her skull. Kim felt just the same. She should have known better. Nothing was ever as pleasant as she imagined it would be.

How long were you together?

That was a hard question to answer. Kim couldn't remember a time Vinh hadn't been in her life, since they'd been in foster care together. For a long time she called him brother until they were twelve and living apart. They were in her room, lying on the bed side by side and reading old comic books they borrowed that morning from the library, when he began kissing her neck, sticking his hands down her shorts, and telling her he loved her. She let him do it, thinking to herself that he smelled different from her foster dads. Dial soap and sour gummy worms and this made her smile and believe this wasn't scary like the other times, and maybe this was how it was supposed to be, this was right.

A while, Kim said. She finished polishing the bracelet she had in her hand, placed it to the side and picked up another.

The woman shook her head as she opened another bottle of jewelry polish. It was after hours, the store lights dimmed, the blinds twisted closed. Kim was helping with the weekly merchandise cleaning. A cassette of old Vietnamese folk music, songs Kim vaguely remembered from old foster homes, played softly from a boom box behind the counter.

You're too young to have a serious boyfriend, the woman said. It only causes trouble.

You think?

Oh, I know, believe me.

Kim regarded her carefully. So you waited to get married.

Yes. I was nearly thirty, and I was fine with it.

What about children?

The woman worked hard trying to rub out some invisible speck of dirt from an earring. After she was satisfied she looked up. I don't think so, she said. I never thought I would make a good mother.

Kim glanced at the recently polished jewelry piled neatly on the counter. Her exaggerated reflection appeared in one of the fatter earrings. She looked so serious. Me neither, Kim said.

Oh don't say that, the woman said. You're young. You don't know yet.

When did you know?

The woman shrugged. I'm not sure. I think I always did. She looked at Kim's hands and smiled. You like that bracelet.

Kim set it down quickly.

Do you want it?

Kim hesitated. I can't afford it.

I know, you're saving up for the apartment. Take it, a gift from me.

Kim didn't move.

Take it, the woman said again, picking up the bracelet and pressing it into Kim's hands. Think of it as an early birthday present, okay?

Kim stared at her, stunned. She didn't remember telling the woman her birthday was coming up. Only a slight struggle, and together they pushed the bracelet over the wrist bone of Kim's left hand.

See? the woman said, as they both admired the pale sea green of the jade. It's lovely.

Kim hadn't seen the social worker since her emancipation last year. They didn't part on the best of terms. The social worker wanted Kim to stay in her last foster home until the end of the school year to make sure she graduated from high school. But Kim already knew from her grades fall semester there was no point. The social worker warned Kim she would regret it.

No one will hire you, she said. You won't have any kind of future.

The social worker didn't get it. Kim had seen enough foster kids after their emancipation and graduation from high school. Little difference between them and the dropouts. Kim didn't need the extra headache. She also couldn't bear another day with her foster parents and knew they felt the same. For her eighteenth birthday, her foster mother gave her a fifty-dollar bill and an old suitcase. You're an adult now, she said. Don't do anything stupid.

That part of Kim's life was behind her. Except for her old foster brothers and sisters, she wanted nothing to do with the rest, the adults who were supposed to look after her and instead screwed everything up. Especially the social worker. Kim used to wonder if the woman had done it on purpose: found the most inappropriate homes to put her in as punishment for a crime Kim didn't know she'd committed. Most of the other Babylift orphans had turned out okay, stayed in the adoptive homes assigned to them. They weren't returned, like Kim was. Now, looking at the social worker, slightly plump in the hips, wide eyes that blinked too often and seemed to comprehend little, a dumb smile that materialized too quickly, Kim realized it was just incompetence.

The social worker tried to hug her when she first entered the room, a small un-air-conditioned cubicle in the corner of a cramped office building across the street from the police station and juvenile detention area. She let go when she didn't feel Kim's arms reach up to complete the hug. The woman had briefly forgotten. Kim didn't like to be touched.

I want to see my file, Kim said.

The social worker looked her over, and Kim stared right back. She'd dressed up in one of Mai's blouses and skirts for the visit, not to impress her or anything, but to ward off any pointed questions and smug assumptions.

What do you want to know? the social worker asked.

My parents.

Kim. I told you before there are private agencies you can go to if you want to try to find your American father.

Kim shook her head. I don't care about my father. I want to know about my mother.

The social worker shuffled some of the papers on her desk, which Kim remembered as the woman's way of looking busy, important.

I don't know if we have anything on her, she said, but I'll pull up your file, and we can look it over together next week.

Why not now?

I have a meeting in a half hour. And your file isn't in this building anymore. I need to get it from the archives.

Only a year and she was already in the archives. Kim suddenly felt old.

I can't promise you anything, the social worker said, as Kim stood up to leave. You know that, right?

I know, Kim said. She kept herself from reminding the social worker she never could, but Kim knew that would only be spiteful. It surprised Kim, how thoughtful that was. She never would have held her tongue a year ago. Maybe she was growing.

The money Kim had been counting on for the rent deposit was gone. It would take another month's wages to get it back, but the apartment Kim wanted needed a security deposit by tomorrow or they'd rent it to somebody else. Kim needed the money now.

Where is it all going? Mai asked. I thought you were trying to save up.

I am, Kim said. I needed it for a doctor's appointment.

They were at Pho Gia-Dinh, their favorite restaurant for lunch—Mai's treat. The place was shutting down next month.

With plastic tables, metal foldout chairs, and walls sticky with mildew, Pho Gia-Dinh couldn't compete with the newer, more modern noodle shops opening up in Little Saigon that offered bilingual menus and fresh flowers on neatly ironed linen tablecloths.

Little Saigon was changing, outgrowing the pagoda-style shopping centers and replacing them with spacious indoor, multilevel malls. The newest one that opened last month boasted four levels and a giant concrete Buddha squatting between two gleaming red pillars with a water fountain courtyard. Kim wasn't so impressed with the new development if it meant her favorite restaurant couldn't survive. They'd been going to Pho Gia-Dinh for years, since they were old enough to scrape together three dollars to share a bowl of pho.

You'll never have enough for a place if you don't save, Mai said, before slurping up a spoonful of noodles.

Mai talked like she knew about money problems. She never understood how lucky she was to have foster parents who gave her an allowance, who never called her a financial burden, keeping a running list of her food and clothing costs.

I need a second job, Kim said.

You work forty hours at the restaurant.

I'll cut down, Kim said. I need to find something that pays better anyway. She felt tired thinking about it. She hated her job, but was due for a raise in two months. She couldn't afford to leave.

Vinh wouldn't really kick you out, Mai said.

Kim stirred the spoon in her near-empty bowl, first clockwise, then the other way. Sipping the leftover broth, partially cooled with tiny bits of beef floating in it, was always her favorite part of the meal. But Kim couldn't finish this time.

From the beginning Mai had disapproved of Kim living

with Vinh. Mai and Vinh had hated each other since they were kids. He was a bully, and she was a crybaby. In their second foster home together, Mai had tattled on Vinh for punching her in the stomach after a fight about Popsicle colors. The social worker promptly transferred Vinh to another home, permanently separating him from Kim and Mai. Vinh had never forgiven Mai. Kim couldn't really blame him. The social worker had always preferred Mai, felt sorry for her, placing her in better homes, while Vinh and Kim were treated like afterthoughts. Kim would always share that with Vinh.

The social worker had called yesterday, saying she couldn't find anything on Kim's mother. Kim shouldn't have been surprised. The woman probably hadn't even looked that hard. She thought Kim had blown her future long ago, squandered her opportunity to have an American family. Kim didn't know why the Johnsons had returned her to social services after only a month. She'd only been three years old. But she must have done something wrong. It was too long ago to remember what.

Vinh always said he was glad the Johnsons had given her up. He never would have known her if they hadn't.

I can't stay there, Kim said. She didn't want him to hate her, and that would happen if she stayed. She'd screwed things up so badly. She never should have moved in with Vinh, or let him fuck her out of gratitude. Another lesson learned the difficult and expensive way. She had to use her current paycheck for the abortion. But she still needed to get away from Vinh.

I have to get that apartment.

Where are you going to get four hundred dollars? Mai asked.

After lunch, Kim and Mai walked to the bus stop. Mai's

arrived first, and they said good-bye, promising to call each other later. Five minutes later, Kim's bus approached, but she waved it by. She did the same with the second one. After a half hour of this, she finally stood up and started walking toward Magnolia.

There were several customers in the store so Kim waited until they finished their shopping and left.

The woman smiled in greeting, but when she saw Kim's face, her forehead creased with concern. Kim relaxed slightly at this, knowing this woman cared about her welfare, wouldn't turn her back on her.

What's the matter?

I need four hundred dollars, Kim said. By tomorrow.

Why? Are you in some kind of trouble?

It's for the apartment, Kim said.

What happened to the money you were saving up?

It's gone, Kim said. Please, you have to help me.

I don't have that kind of money to give out.

Yes you do, I've seen it in the register, and there's lots more in the safe.

The woman's eyes narrowed. This is inappropriate. I can't give you any of that money.

Why not?

You're practically a stranger.

I am not.

Yes, you are.

Then why did you give this to me? Kim asked, holding up her bracelet. I know you only give this to family. Mothers to daughters, I know.

But the woman shook her head, her face located somewhere between confusion and disgust.

I gave that to you because I felt sorry for you, the woman said slowly, like she was talking to someone she hadn't been getting to know for the last three weeks. You kept staring at it so pitifully. That's all.

Kim stared at her, conscious through every blink of her eyes the woman was changing into something else. Once familiar, the woman became a stranger again. Her features were not so similar to Kim's, her face, body language not so loving. She'd been wrong. Kim hated being wrong.

Abruptly, she turned to walk out of the store, half-hoping the woman would call out to her, say something to stop her. But all Kim heard was the faint music from the store, the buzz of the air-conditioning, and the bells of the door as she pushed it open and stepped out.

The jade bracelet had grown tight around her wrist, cutting off circulation, so she squeezed it off and threw it across the bedroom when she got home. Five minutes later, she couldn't find it. She tore up the room, searching everywhere, but it was no use.

When Vinh came home, he found her knotted up on the floor.

His hands held her face still, his eyes searching her body for any obvious injuries.

What happened? Vinh asked. Who hurt you?

Bitch, that goddamned bitch.

Who?

She didn't want me then and now, even now.

What are you talking about?

Kim remembered that first day they met, when the woman caught her stealing.

Thief, Kim said. She always thought that. I was nothing more to her.

Who? Vinh was shaking her shoulders. Who called you a thief?

Kim finally met Vinh's gaze. She thought of the first time Vinh discovered her bruises. The night Kim ran away to his house and finally told him about her foster father. That really bad summer before high school when they wanted to run away together. So much she tried not to think about, tried to forget, because it hurt that she was so weak, vulnerable, stupid, and she wanted to change and be a completely different person. She never would be able to get away from that nervous, trembling child, because she was still her, still a huge, broken part of her that she could never ignore, not completely anyway. Because of the way Vinh looked at her since they were kids, and still looked at her. Because he knew what she meant when she couldn't get the words right. Because he saw all of it. He knew too much, and still it was okay.

Mekong Gifts, Kim said. A few blocks off Magnolia. Under the counter, behind the Buddha statues. It's a combination lock.

Vinh nodded. He was blinking too much, like he was trying to hide something, rage, obviously, but also excitement. It had been a long time since Kim had requested anything of him. He did not intend to let her down.

He moved her to the bed and Kim turned her swollen face into the musty sheets, half-listening to Vinh on the phone, summoning the other boys. She reached for a pillow, sticking her head inside the case like a mask. The weave of the thin pillowcase wasn't tight enough, sunlight penetrating from the room's single naked window.

People never tired of asking her. Don't you want to know about your American father? You look so much like him. Maybe he's looking for you. Maybe he wants you. Maybe he's rich.

Kim wasn't like the other orphans. Neither was Vinh. They never cried at night thinking about their missing/dead/run-away parents. They didn't create elaborate excuses for their absence. Their parents were gone. And there was nothing they could do to change that.

Kim had forgotten that for a while. She'd forgotten many things. Trying to find something else, she'd rejected what she did have. She should have known no one would ever know her like Vinh.

She heard the front door slam, then quiet. Kim lay still and listened to the footsteps jogging down the stairs to the drive-way below, the slamming of the car door, the engine starting, and Vinh driving away to meet the others. She imagined what Vinh would say to the other members before the attack: disre-spect, regaining honor, teaching that woman a lesson, no one fucks with 354. Over the years Vinh had learned what moti-vated his boys, what pushed away their doubts about the things they did, what replaced fear with indignation and anger.

These weren't bad boys. Kim had known most of them since they were kids. Though they all had problems, most were friendly, funny, loyal. The only reason they could do the things they did was because they felt they had to. For years they'd been denied so much from their new country and government-issued families. They robbed these houses and stores to break even, to survive. They believed they had no other choice.

Most of the people they attacked were men. To rob a woman, Vinh would have to convince them she was even worse. He could do it, too, Kim had seen him do it. He'd turn her into every foster mother, every teacher, every boss who once sneered at them, who told them they'd turn out to be nothing. And now look: they weren't nothing. They were 354. They'd show her.

They'd walk into the store without stopping, scratching their wool masks from Kmart, scuffing their sneakers on the linoleum. The bells on the door would jingle, and someone would tear them off, throwing them to the floor. They'd smash the glass counters, clear off shelves. Someone would get to the register. Two others would start working on the safe. They'd see the woman, her panicked expression, and mistake it for scorn. Someone would pull out a gun, but Vinh would look out the window, checking, and yell at them, *not yet*.

And then. And then Kim didn't know. She didn't know what they would do next. She sat up. It crept through her so slowly and thoroughly, from deep in her stomach up her neck to the strands of her hair, the realization of what she'd just done. Vinh never really told Kim what they did with the merchants and families they robbed. She was certain they weren't left untouched. The boys weren't only out for money. They wanted to give back their pain.

Kim lunged across the mattress, reaching under the bed for the phone. She punched in Vinh's beeper number, waited for the signal, then dialed in their home number. She hung up and waited. And waited. She paged him again, this time punching in 911 at the end. Five minutes passed, and he hadn't called back. She tried again. Ten more minutes. Again. The same thing.

Still, Kim didn't get it. She sat on that bed, dialing and waiting, dialing and waiting, her hand slippery from its tight, sweaty grip on the receiver. Not yet, not yet, she thought, still convinced she could undo what was happening while she sat on the bed, waiting, waiting.

THE

DELTA

THE CONVENT HADN'T ABSORBED her completely. Silky strands of dark hair escaped from underneath her black habit. The eyes, now burdened with heavy bags and shadows, nevertheless appeared bright and sharp. A deceptively diminutive gold cross lay between her heavily cloaked breasts. A clumsy, unabashed smile dominated her delicate face. The loveliest thing he'd ever looked at. Truc hadn't seen Phuong in twelve years.

You don't greet old friends? she asked, her deep voice unaltered, though now it seemed too flirtatious for a woman of the cloth to possess.

Truc stepped forward and dutifully kissed Phuong on the cheek, deliberately restraining himself from inhaling her scent. He didn't have to know if that remained the same or not.

How is your health? Truc asked. It was customary to inquire of one's well-being, though Truc had asked, not to be polite, but to make a point. There was a time when such formalities between them were unnecessary.

Fine. Her face softened into a more amused expression. And yours?

Truc shrugged. I have no complaints.

She stared at him hard, doubtfully. Then she took a step back, her eyes drifting to the dusty floor, once again the humble nun. Please come in.

Truc stepped in, enjoying the chill of the sweat coating his back. The insulation from the convent's cement walls was almost as invaluable as an electric fan during the Delta summers. Though open-air, the atrium was protected with large shade trees above. He looked around the room. Empty except for a thick wooden cross hanging in the afternoon shadows.

Was it a long drive? Phuong asked.

No. Your brother gave good directions.

We're still practically neighbors then. Her expression was sad, as though the knowledge that they still lived within a reasonable distance from each other but he never thought to visit was a rejection.

Come with me, Phuong said, walking through the atrium to another door.

Where are we going? Truc asked, peering over Phuong's shoulder as he followed behind.

I want you to meet them first.

He didn't take the afternoon off to chat with the rest of the sisters. He was hoping they'd have a chance to catch up privately, give her an opportunity to explain the last twelve years.

But they weren't alone. Their two sets of footsteps echoing through the hall were soon joined by solemn murmurs, other footsteps, and, finally, crying. Individual wails of despair, anger, and naked panic. Babies.

I didn't realize this was also an orphanage. Truc stood behind Phuong in a large room crammed with wooden cribs.

Several sisters hunched over beds where the loudest wails originated. There were four or five infants tangled in every crib. Smells of urine and feces mingled in the stale air.

It wasn't, Phuong said. A few years ago the Immaculate Souls orphanage grew overcrowded, so we volunteered to open up some empty rooms here. Now we shelter more infants than they do.

Truc should have realized. It was probably Phuong's idea. When they were children, she could hear her younger cousins crying from across the river.

She stepped forward to the nearest crib and gathered one of the babies in her arms. The little girl struggled to hold her head up, blinking away the flies surrounding her eyes and nose. A cloth diaper hung loosely on her. Harsh red boils overwhelmed her bony arms and legs. Truc fought the impulse to recoil.

This one we named Hanh because she came to us so delicate. Not that the others weren't either. Most are malnourished when they are brought here.

Truc thought of his nieces and nephews when they were first born, their chubby, petal-soft skin blushing with health and vigor. These babies burned red for another reason. Those without boils appeared transparent, disappearing into the thin gray sheets they lay on. There were so many of them.

Hanh squirmed in Phuong's arms, wrinkled eyes and crumpled face, but nothing came forth, sound or matter, from her open mouth. Phuong laid her back down and pulled a formula bottle from the corner of the crib to fit between Hanh's shaking lips.

It's watered down. The more babies we get, the thinner we have to cut the milk and—

What is this? Truc said. Why did you bring me here?

Phuong breathed evenly, as if she expected this kind of reaction from him. My brother said your family had an automobile.

Truc nodded.

They'd bought it several years ago for transporting produce. Truc and his brother traveled to Saigon once a week to sell ducks and eggs at the Cholon market.

There's an orphanage in Saigon with more facilities and resources than we have here. They're willing to take ten of our infants. Truc waved away a fly. He should have expected this. You want a ride.

We lose children every day from infections. There were two epidemics of measles in the last year, and last month we lost twelve babies to chicken pox. We have a chance to save some of them.

The pungent air was overwhelming him. Truc tried to breathe through his mouth. He felt the floor beneath him slip a little, but was afraid of touching anything to regain balance. He thought of his science classes in high school. He thought of the germs.

You need to think about this, Phuong said, her voice as smooth as the patient expression on her face. I understand. If you decide you want to help us, you can tell my brother.

One of the babies started screeching above the others. Truc turned to leave. As he walked out, he saw Phuong lift the screaming infant to her chest. But instead of rocking the child back and forth or caressing its back, she simply pulled the baby's diaper away, realized it didn't need changing, and promptly returned it to the crib. Truc jolted in shock, but quickly tried to dismiss it. Stepping out of the door, he could hear the child's gulping screams bounce off the walls, lingering in his ears, until he reached the end of the hall, opened the heavy front door, and closed it behind him.

They first held hands when they were three years old. She was crying, and he wanted to know why.

It bit me, she said, pointing to a large suspicious duck nibbling at a grass weed in the pond. Her hair gleamed in the orange air of dusk, her tear-stained cheeks glowed pink.

Truc chased after the boorish bird, dodging the tall lime grass slapping in his face, determined to make it pay. The duck honked hysterically as it flapped away, alerting Truc's father. He ran toward the pond and picked up his incensed son, slightly amused at the boy's righteous anger.

It hurt Phuong, Truc said, still glaring over his father's shoulder at the guilty creature.

Their families laughed over this, recounted it again and again over suppers and holidays, Truc's heroic protection of Phuong at such a young age.

He loved her before he knew he was supposed to, Truc's mother had said, nodding in complete assurance.

Though their engagement wasn't official until after Phuong's fifteenth birthday—a large celebration also honoring Tet with half the village in attendance—both families knew their youngest children were intended for each other. Truc's family had been sending their ducks to feed in Phuong's family's rice paddies for years, a symbiotic relationship that nourished their birds while ridding the paddies of harmful insects. It seemed natural to merge the farms together through their children. They even joked that Phuong's mother had intentionally become pregnant after Truc's mother announced her expectancy. They all agreed: Phuong was created for Truc.

They're paying premium, Mother, Truc said. Some wedding banquet.

But only twenty-five birds? His mother fretted as Truc and several servants struggled to tie the birds' feet together for the trip. It was just after dawn, the land still quiet except for the occasional whispers of insects. Phuong had wanted to leave as early as possible to protect the babies from most of the day's heat. His mother clucked at the small number of ducks. Is the trip worth it?

It's good money. And I already promised the bride's father.

But Sao and Anh will be fine by themselves? On days Truc didn't regularly travel to Saigon they sold ducks and eggs in the local floating market in Can Tho.

They're loading the sampan as we speak. You know we can trust them.

She nodded, her lips still bunched together in doubt. I know, I know. What you think is best. Since his father's death and his older brothers' departures to join the liberation front, the farm had become Truc's responsibility. His mother helped out occasionally, but spent most of her time at the ancestors' altar burning incense for the unification of Vietnam and her sons' safe return home. She depended solely on Truc, supported almost every decision he made, except his stubborn determination to remain a bachelor. And that she protested in silence.

Truc angled the cages on top of each other, pushing them as far against the walls as possible. It would be crowded, but there was no choice. The birds had to come to avoid suspicion.

They were waiting for him in front of the convent. Not just Phuong and the chosen infants, but what seemed like the entire orphanage. Shuffling their feet in the dust and peering around like they were waiting to have their picture taken. It was an awkward reception. There were those who recognized Truc and avoided eye contact, unsure of his temperament. Those who didn't know Truc gazed upon him with gratitude. The children were of varying sizes, the older ones holding smaller infants, looking on him with a mixture of suspicion and longing.

Truc took his time getting out of the van, letting his feet sink into the muddy soil until he felt it stabilize. Several children encircled him. He didn't take any of their outstretched hands, waving his own high up in the air, trying to smile and not look terrified.

He unlatched the van doors. Feathers sailed out, drifted along the ground, luring a few young boys and girls to chase after them. The ducks flapped their wings as sunlight streamed in and started to quack at the children exclaiming over them. Phuong, holding a small baby swaddled tightly in a stained pink blanket, stared at the birds uncertainly.

Those are coming with us?

It'll be fine. I'll lock the cages.

Two sisters laid out several blankets on the van floor. Others carried wooden crates and cardboard boxes—makeshift cribs—into the van. The ducks stared at the tiny orphans with interest, tapping their yellow bills against the cages.

Phuong introduced Truc to each baby. She looked at him each time, perhaps expecting him to pick up their tiny grubby bodies and kiss them hello. The infants chosen to travel to Saigon had survived last month's chicken pox epidemic, but were still frail enough that their survival depended on better nutrition and more individual care. Several were Amerasian, bastards of the American soldiers, both black and white. Probably from rape. Truc tried to look at them with sympathy. It was not their fault. Just innocent babies. Phuong said their only chance was international adoption in America or Australia. They could never have a life here.

The orange streaks in the sky were brightening, chasing the morning mist away. Truc offered Phuong an old stool so she could sit in back with the babies, but she wanted to sit in front.

They'll be fine. If there's a problem, I'll just crawl back there.

With the cargo settled in, Truc started the motor. Phuong sat next to him only an arm's length away. Her feet as a child were always bare, but now they were cloaked in scuffed black shoes, crossed at the ankles. Her habit was smoothed straight behind her shoulders. Her hands folded neatly in her lap. Phuong looked tired, her eyes drifting closed until the van jotted over a bump, and they fluttered open again.

Usually Truc had one of the servants accompany him on the drive to Saigon and they'd chat about business or village gossip. But Phuong didn't seem in the mood to talk, and Truc didn't know what to say to her. He looked as far ahead as he could, his eyes drifting over the wood-thatched huts along the road, the ancestral tombs dotting the rice paddies. He glanced in the side mirror at the children playing in the roadside dust they left behind. He noted the growing heat emanating through the automobile's metal roof and decided to roll the window open.

After realizing with relief how serene the ride had been so far, Truc jerked as one of the babies began to cry defiantly, provoking the ducks to react. Truc sternly quieted the birds. Phuong crawled to the back and after a few seconds, presumably after giving the child a bottle, returned to her seat. But the infant was still crying. Truc peered over at Phuong, who was facing out her window.

Phuong.

It'll be all right. She didn't turn around.

The child continued to cry. Truc tried to concentrate on driving, the ball of his foot gauging the pedals, his hands clenching the sweaty, slippery steering wheel.

Phuong.

Just wait a minute.

They did. Eventually, the baby offered a final pathetic howl and fell silent, waiting, then, nothing, presumably falling asleep again.

You have to do that, Phuong said, glancing over at him, smiling sleepily. You have to wait.

Truc nodded. These were not his children. It was not up to him to judge what was cruel or not.

A purr of contentment drifted from Phuong's side of the car.

Truc looked over to her window. What?

In the glass reflection, Phuong's eyes absorbed the banana palms along the burnt muddy waters of the river. She turned over to Truc's side to concentrate on the rich green rice paddies. We hardly have the opportunity to leave the grounds, she said. I still live here, but not really. I forgot how beautiful the Delta is.

Truc returned his eyes to the road. You don't visit home?

I haven't been back since I left. She shifted in her seat. You know that.

He did. He just wanted to hear her say it.

Truc was in bed for a week after Phuong broke their engagement, suffering from a phlegmy, bloody cough originating deep from within his chest. He'd been relatively healthy as a child, no serious illnesses or broken bones, but Phuong's departure seemed to inspire his immune system to abandon him also. For the next few months, he couldn't be seen out of his pajamas, since he was catching any virus or disease floating around the village. The illnesses were soon replaced with chronic insomnia, compelling Truc to take long walks on the farm at night with an oil lamp to guide him. He awoke the ducks with his soft steps, and they'd waddle from their unlocked wire cages, following behind, keeping him company.

He's worried about the government, his mother would tell her friends, slightly embarrassed at having a son who'd mourn a broken relationship for so long. He doesn't trust those Catholic brutes.

Initially the family indulged Truc's shattered heart and its strange manifestations. But they were getting complaints from the neighbors that the ducks were keeping them awake at night. He fell asleep at inopportune moments, during worshiping or supper. In the fall, Truc decided not to return to Saigon to finish his last year of school. He didn't know when he would be ready to complete his studies.

You need something to do, Truc's father said. You're going to work on the farm. The ducks already like you.

And they did. Truc became responsible for coaxing the ducklings out of their shells, and when he'd gathered them together for feeding time on the rice paddies, they'd prod his hands with their golden bills, smoothing their feathers along his pants. This worried Truc, especially when his father and older brothers demanded he learn to kill and gut the birds so he could help sell them at the open market.

One humid afternoon Truc's older brother Binh finally forced him to sit outside one of the cages and do it. One of the ducks calmly moved in front of them and settled near Truc's feet.

It's just a stupid bird. It was born to die. Now put your hands around its neck. Lock your fingers together. That's it. Now squeeze. See how their eyes pop from the sockets a bit? That's how you know it's working. Keep going. Harder, Truc. Do it fast, you just have to break it, it's easier that way. See how the eyes are getting glassy? See how you can tell by looking in their eyes?

Truc's grip held tight, his gaze locked onto the bird's. Like Phuong's eyes, so dark and wide and hard you wondered what thoughts cowered behind them.

The skinny two-lane road was growing crowded. Truc eased his foot on the brake and frowned. He rarely encountered traffic at this time. He cleared his throat from the idle car exhaust swelling in front of them. Now they sat at a standstill.

Poking his head out the window, Truc found the problem: three dark green military tanks encamped on the roadside with matching soldiers, unsmiling, hugging their guns protectively against their chests. He settled back in his seat. Perfect. They stumbled upon a checkpoint. These routine inspections could take hours.

Every so often a car in the opposite lane would pass, and Truc wondered if he should just turn around and find an alternate route. But there was no room, and now there were soldiers dispersed evenly along the road. Truc waved at one of them until he finally walked over.

Are you closing this road?

The South Vietnamese soldier was a kid, probably no older than eighteen. Uh. He looked around for his superiors, but they were too far off to catch his pleading eyes. He looked back at Truc. Yes.

When were you going to tell us?

Truc, Phuong whispered.

The boy looked stunned by the sudden disrespect and narrowed his eyes. We're following protocol.

You need to explain to each automobile one at a time that the road is closed?

This is protocol.

Truc. Phuong's voice was stern this time, the model nun.

It's stupid. Can I just turn around?

Um. The soldier bit his lip. No.

Why not?

What do you have back there? The soldier peered over Truc's shoulder.

Ducks and babies.

The soldier held his gun up higher. Open the back, sir.

I've got a nun sitting next to me. Do you really think I'm VC?

Truc! Phuong glared at him. That's enough. Just do what he says.

Rolling his eyes, Truc stepped out of the van. I'd hardly think President Diem would have approved.

Once the soldiers inspected the van, Truc and Phuong were released, with a few snide remarks about selling ducks and babies, to turn the automobile around and leave. Truc impatiently pressed on the gas, the tires spinning briefly, trying to make up for the lost time. Since his usual route was closed, they'd have to take the ferry over. He hated the ferry.

Phuong's arms crossed in front of her chest. Tiny beads of sweat sprang in a row along her scalp, but she made no move to roll down her window. Truc suspected this silence was different from her earlier one, more deliberate and pointed against him.

What's wrong? Truc finally asked, resenting that nothing had really changed, that he'd once again succumbed to Phuong's sulky tantrum like he did when they were children.

Why did you have to bring up Diem? You knew they'd have to search the van.

I'm sorry. Did I offend your god by speaking badly of the late honorable president? Are you afraid I'm going to, what is it, hell? Eternal damnation?

Her exhale of breath lasted significantly, like she'd been holding it in most of the morning. Phuong looked at him with more annoyance than hurt. It isn't the Lord's fault.

Truc swerved to avoid an oblivious, possibly blind, dog wandering across the road. Your lord is tearing our country apart.

Phuong was staring at her feet, shaking her head. This was not the girl who was once his fiancée, the one who would never let him push her around so easily. Finally, she looked at him. The Lord would not condone what has happened to our country, she said, her voice trying hard not to vibrate. No God would.

Did you know my father died?

Phuong hesitated. Yes. Her chin pointed to her chest, her gold cross. My brother told me.

Do you know why?

She took even longer to answer this one. He could barely

hear her, like she could mollify the past with softness. He spoke out against the government.

Maybe you should have thought of that before asking me for this favor.

You were the only one I knew with an automobile. We were desperate. She closed her eyes. If it meant you could help these children, I was willing to let you hate me a little more.

As the youngest children of prosperous families, it would have been easy for Truc and Phuong to grow up as spoiled and sheltered as other landowners' children. But their families, who understood that wealth was a rare blessing in their country, refused to hide the war from them. They had long agreed that their children needed to understand the land they lived in and the poverty that most of their countrymen suffered. As soon as Truc and Phuong could walk steadily, they began tagging along with their grandmothers and older siblings to take leftover rice and duck meat to the poor in the village slums.

The first afternoon, Truc's grandmother urged him to knock on the doors of the small bamboo huts along the river, while she and the others stood behind him. Initially he was terrified, wanting only to hide behind his older brothers' legs. But the families took the sacks from Truc's arms gratefully, and after setting them aside, the women rubbed their hands and lips all over his face and hair, profusely expressing their appreciation. He endured these affectionate displays as best he could.

Phuong had been quiet for most of the afternoon, unusual for the girl who could never stop chatting or wiggling during worship in the pagoda. Truc realized the problem when they arrived at the shack of a widow. Several naked babies lay on the dirt floor, their misleadingly rotund stomachs full of emptiness, limbs as narrow as grass weed in the wind. They stared up at the strangers, too weak to vocalize any emotion.

She stood in the doorway, staring at those babies, as their families brushed past her. Truc touched her arm to help her inside, and she recoiled from him.

Don't do that, she said.

What? Truc asked, confused.

Just don't. Her eyes moistened and Truc fearfully backed away.

Her older brothers and sister had tried to coax Phuong inside, but she howled in protest, screaming that she wanted to go home. When they finally agreed to head back, she couldn't even walk by herself. Her brother Ngo had to carry her.

Her parents remained adamant she continue the trips to the slums, hoping Phuong would grow out of this behavior. Phuong never got used to it. She couldn't look at an emaciated child without crying. Truc was so disturbed by her hysterical reactions that he attempted to hide those sickly babies from her whenever they were near, diverting her attention, standing in the way. But she eventually sought these children out, as though she was growing to enjoy the pain they caused her, an empathy she wasn't used to and realized she needed.

Their families believed her behavior a sign of Phuong's destined success for motherhood, and when their children grew older, often teased Truc and Phuong that they must wait until after the marriage ceremony to create babies. Then, Phuong's mother had said, her betel-blackened teeth peeking out from her sly, thin lips, you can have as many as you want, no complaints from me.

The road to the ferry was more neglected than the direct route to Saigon, constricted and bumpier, with sharp turns and sudden drops. Truc navigated through these obstacles with caution, fearing to provoke the babies awake. But even when the road had calmed to fine, damp dirt, the babies were still fussing. Initially there were only a few muted cries of frustration and discomfort, but soon nearly all the children were crying steadily, doggedly.

Eventually Phuong crawled back to stay with them. Still, their uneasiness would not abate. Several infants began screaming, their piercing cries bouncing off the van's metal walls, encouraging the ducks to join in, flapping hysterically.

Phuong returned to her seat. They're hungry. It's their nursing time.

Did you feed them?

I gave them water. But they're hungry for milk.

You didn't bring any milk? Truc swerved the car to the right, achieving his impulse to also knock Phuong against her side door, which, fortunately, was locked. She pulled herself back in her seat shakily, her hands struggling to smooth out her habit, her composure. She looked behind to make sure the infants still lay in their cribs.

Why?

We couldn't afford to bring formula in case it spoiled, so we brought water instead. We fed them right before we left.

He shook his head, unable even to look at her. Maybe it's a good thing we didn't marry and have children, Truc said as he put the car in reverse. You may be a servant of your Catholic god, but there is no compassion in you. Letting babies starve like this, you could never be a good mother.

She did not respond until she realized they had turned off the main road. Where are we going?

We're getting milk.

No one had thought much of Phuong's volunteer work at the new clinic. If anything, they found it noble, so typical of their sweet, concerned girl. It didn't seem important that the clinic was founded by an order of nuns who'd fled from the North after the Demarcation. Though aware of the many pagodas and communal houses in the Delta, the sisters still wanted to establish the clinic, which they felt was needed in a village with only two midwives. At least they're doing something good, many villagers had pointed out. No one else wanted to do it.

The nuns seemed polite and good-natured, wearing the classic black-and-white habits and wooden rosaries the villagers had seen at the cinema and associated with the Catholics. Their enthusiasm attracted an admiring following, including Phuong. She'd long been disappointed by the Buddhist monks in their village, who, Phuong believed, did little except remain cloistered in their pagodas to meditate.

They only come out to collect food donations for themselves and take away food from the poor, Phuong said. What are they doing to help the community?

They're worshiping for us while we work, Truc said. That's what they're called to do.

Phuong shook her head. It's a waste.

Truc liked that the nuns kept Phuong busy. She'd taken his departure to secondary school in Saigon very badly. She'd wanted to go away to school with him, but her parents believed that a higher education was a waste for a girl who already possessed her farm skills. She was needed on their rice paddies. Phuong couldn't be found the morning Truc left for his first year of school. She later confessed she'd stayed hidden on purpose.

I thought I could make you stay if you couldn't find me, Phuong said. They lay together in the spare room in the servants' quarters, where no one could disturb them. Because how could you leave without saying good-bye to me?

They had never before doubted their future together, but with Truc living in Saigon during the week, Phuong loudly expressed her worries. There were so many pretty, educated girls in the city. Truc tried to assure her his only thoughts in Saigon were of her and the war. They realized how petty some of their concerns were. Their countrymen were dying, steadily, and they worried only about each other.

The clinic posed as an ideal alternative for Phuong. She spoke often of the innovations—the sisters knew about vaccinations, proper hygiene, and prenatal care. She introduced Truc to the nuns, who innocently bowed to him and spoke of the pleasant weather. It seemed a harmless hobby to Truc. One that kept her busy and made her feel necessary. For this, Truc was appreciative of the nuns.

At the closest town, Truc stopped at the local open-air market and negotiated a trade for several bottles of rice milk. Grabbing one of the ducks from the cages, Truc swiftly broke its neck, and plucked and gutted the bird in front of Phuong and the street vendor. Wiping the blood on his pants, he shoved the bottles, sticky with sweat and entrails, into Phuong's hands. It was the first time he'd touched her all day.

Go pour them in the bottles.

Truc thought he must have surprised Phuong when he revealed he intended to help feed the babies. He knew there was no choice since they'd already lost so much time. They sat across from each other in the back of the van, pulling a baby into each of their laps.

There was a layer of fabric between him and the child. Truc reminded himself of this constantly when picking up the first one. The baby howled at first contact, like he could sense Truc's revulsion. He tried to nudge the boy's mouth open to suckle the plastic nipple, even impatiently reminding the child he was starving; but the baby refused to be fed, screaming every time the nipple tapped his lips.

He knows you don't want to do this, Phuong finally said, scooting to Truc's side. Here. She showed him how to cradle the infant and, with the thumb and index fingers pressing on the child's cheeks, prod the mouth open and fit the bottle in.

After the first few feedings, Truc relaxed into its natural rhythm, allowing it to calm him. He noted how each child delighted in receiving food, eagerly swallowing the milk and burping with satisfaction. He suddenly realized the magnitude of the babies' unease this day, stuffed in boxes or crates, enduring bumps in the road and the loud company of the ducks. He congratulated those who finished their bottles without much fuss. He even managed to caress their cheeks and soothe their cries with a low, assuring voice.

He lulled the last child to sleep, until it softly snored through its nostrils and closed-bud mouth. After he eased the infant back into the cardboard box, he turned and saw Phuong crouching in the corner of the van, staring at him. When she realized she had his attention, she looked away.

That one you were just holding, I found him on our doorstep. Phuong rested her head against the van wall. I answered the door that morning. The mother had run away.

But I thought I could feel her nearby, hiding and watching us. So I waited for her to come out. I wanted to give her a chance to see the people who she was giving her baby to.

He knew he wasn't supposed to say anything, so he didn't. He'd begun to regret some of the words he'd said. Resettling his legs into a more comfortable position, Truc waited for her to speak again.

They drop them off every day, she said. Sometimes two in a day. Sometimes they hand us the baby, upset, even angry, and explain their situations. But most we never see. They just leave them at the door to cry.

Truc tried to meet her eyes; but she was determined not to let him, concentrating on something else, beyond him, the babies and the van. It frightened him how easily she could remove herself from his presence when they were together. It always had.

They never stop coming. They arrive sick, and most of them die with us. After a while, you can't bear holding them in your arms, knowing there's nothing you can do. It is possible to grieve too much. I never thought so before.

Her shoulders were shaking. Truc pulled himself to sit next to her and, hesitantly, awkwardly patted her shoulder, trying to remember how it felt to offer comfort.

No, don't. She pushed his hand away gently, turning her head to the wall. You can't feel sorry for me. I know what I did to you. I won't forget it.

The source of the Mekong River lay in Tibet and traveled over thousands of kilometers through China, Burma, Laos, and Cambodia before entering southern Vietnam. The river nourished the surrounding marshlands and forests, forming the Delta, the river's deposit of the lush soils of so many regions, lands, and people.

Their talks, as they walked along the Delta, often for miles, revolved around fanciful ideas of one day buying a hectare for themselves and creating a legacy apart from what their parents had planned. They prided themselves for having dreams so outrageously against tradition. But they secretly knew it was out of the question. Their families had already paid for a small house to be constructed between their properties, a modest home designed to allow rooms to be added on after children were born. This, they knew, was a generous and lavish wedding gift, since most newlyweds were expected to live in one of the parents' homes and learn to adapt to keeping a large house and caring for the elders. But since their older siblings were already successfully fulfilling those duties, it was decided that Truc and Phuong would be rewarded with their own home for officially uniting the families.

There were some concerns of spending the money on a new house with the war threatening to push its way into the Delta. Truc's father had become sympathetic to the intellectuals in the village who spoke eloquently of the South government's bowing to foreign nations' demands and the necessity of ridding their country of international influences.

We can't survive as two halves, his father often told his family at supper when they discussed political matters, which was becoming more often. Under a puppet government, the South will crumble. We need the North with us.

Though Truc offered to give up the new house, his father still wanted to build it. They will not infect our lives, he'd said. We're going to continue our future. Truc took a leave from school to supervise the house's construction. He'd expected Phuong to be pleased that they would be able to see each other every day for the first time in years, but she'd become busier at the clinic by then, assisting the nuns in birthing infants, and was unable to spend much time with Truc. Initially, he believed this fortuitous. The house would be more of a surprise for her. He devoted every minute he had to preparing the foundation of their new home, thinking, he later realized, foolishly little of his betrothed's increasing distance.

The embarkation zone was clogged with automobiles, bicycles, and people on foot, all struggling to squeeze through, not wanting to wait for the next ferry, which was not due to leave until evening. Truc had enough money to bribe an official for one of the vehicle passes, which supposedly had all been sold. They gingerly drove up the wobbly loading ramp, following the other automobiles onto the wooden ferry. On the main deck, the van was wedged so tightly between a chicken truck and a school bus that they couldn't open the side doors. Then the foot passengers boarded, a noisy cluster of conical hats weaving through the automobiles, congesting the deck further. This was why Truc avoided the ferries.

In the river's brown muddy water, fisherman cast out their nets frantically, hoping to catch the fish attracted to the ferry's motor in time before the boat's departure. A slight breeze floated by, arousing noises of approval and smiles of relief from the ferry passengers. It soon absorbed and disappeared into the heavy, moist air.

The ferry's smokestack exhaled a thick curl of smog followed by a long whistle, indicating departure. Truc and Phuong rolled down their windows and opened the van's back doors to get as much air circulating for the babies as they could. Truc used the blankets the nuns had laid out to fan the infants. But the babies didn't seem to have as much difficulty with the heat as the adults—most of them remained either drowsy or in a contented sleep from their feeding.

Phuong removed her habit so that her arms and calves were bare. Her hair, once down to her waist as Truc last remembered, was now cut above her shoulders.

Don't tell anyone, she said when she caught him staring at her.

Do they know? Truc asked.

What?

That you haven't always been chaste?

It had the desired effect. With shaky hands, she turned away and put her habit back on. He returned to the driver's seat while she remained in the back.

Several street vendors tapped on their van selling baguette sandwiches, fruit, and sugarcane. Truc bought two pâté baguettes and a bag of mango slices. Phuong nibbled on her bread slowly at first, then, realizing her hunger, began tearing into it in large chunks.

From inside the van, they watched the Delta and its inhabitants change. More fishermen, tangled in their nets, arranging baskets of fresh sole, crabs and shrimp in their sampans. Farmers hunched over in rice fields and their children splashing nearby in the lily pads. Two teenage girls swung from a coconut tree, playfully threatening to smash a coconut onto the ferry.

A pair of saffron-shrouded monks waded knee deep in the Delta, splashing their arms and faces to cool off. They waved at the ferry as it passed, smiles as bright as their heads. So different from the photographs Truc saw of them in Saigon newspapers, burning themselves to protest the government's mistreatment of them.

Truc turned to Phuong, still engrossed in her baguette. Do you ever think anything of their suffering?

After following his gaze to the monks, she put down her food. Stop it.

What?

You have to stop blaming the Church for everything wrong. The hardness in her voice from earlier, when the kid soldier had interrogated them, reemerged. The Lord may be perfect, Phuong said, but not his followers. And they shouldn't claim to be either.

But some do.

And I cannot speak for all Catholics. Just me. She looked over to him, finally. And what do you think of their suffering? Or can you only pity the Buddhists? I showed you, Truc. I brought you into our orphanage and showed you what we do every day.

I thought you didn't want me to feel sorry for you.

I'm asking you to consider the other side.

The one you joined?

I do not work for the South Vietnamese. I work for the Lord. I'm not on either government's side.

Truc shook his head at her. Our country is divided. You must take sides.

No.

Do you think the North and South can survive without each other? Don't you want this country to be reunited?

If I thought that would end the suffering, I would. If I believed either of the sides was not corrupt or concerned with its own ambitions, I would take up arms. But they just want to hurt each other. Nothing good will come of this war, except for these babies. If I can help them, then that will be enough for me.

The blow of the ferry's whistle signaled the end of the journey. The captain spoke over the loudspeaker, announcing their impending arrival. Several of the babies awoke and began to cry, agitating the ducks. The van's chorus had returned, and, for the first time that day, Truc felt grateful.

He could feel it through his body, the chill trickling underneath his skin, when she told him they needed to speak privately in the morning, before their families awoke. He couldn't recall the last time she wanted to talk privately with him.

They'd been arguing for months. Truc would try to involve her in the building process, but she seemed uninterested. Then, when she discovered a detail she didn't approve of, she'd become upset, accusing him of creating their home, dictating their future, without her. He knew she argued often with her family about the wedding plans because Phuong's mother told his mother. Words like The Lord and His Mission slipped from her mouth with increasing frequency.

It's those nuns, his mother had said. I knew they'd eventually poison her.

Members of both sides kept pressuring Truc to find out what was wrong with her. Truc had always been the one who could reach her, her confidante, her solace.

She now thought differently. Everyone always assumes you know what I want and what I like, Phuong had said after one particularly bad argument about the distance growing between her and their families. You don't. We do not always like the same things. We never have.

In her family's rice paddies that morning, early enough for no servant to witness, she told him so bluntly and quickly he was convinced it couldn't possibly be her speaking. The words, so cruel and casual, seemed foreign coming from her mouth.

Though embarrassing to acknowledge years later, every plea and entreaty he used to try and change her mind remained as fresh to Truc as the memory of her hand's texture when he used to hold it, or their simultaneous laughter bursting from a silly joke. But while their union provided bittersweet sensations, her rejection was only painful, and his refusal to accept it even more wrenching.

You once thought we were one entity, Truc reminded her. Two persons created for one life.

No, Truc, she said, appearing insulted. It's my life. I choose to give it to the Lord.

Her decision traveled a devastating path. Enraged and humiliated, Truc's family immediately cut off ties with Phuong's family, including business, which soon crippled both houses' incomes. The supplies for the wedding house were used to build a partition between the farms. Truc recalled the ducks' confusion at being chased away from the rice paddies they'd long assumed belonged to them. Truc's father arranged for the ducks to feed at another neighboring rice farm.

People in the village were reluctant to take sides, fearful of having either influential family against them. But the town sentiment eventually turned in favor of Truc's family, especially after the clinic shut down. The sisters decided to move north of the Delta, taking Phuong and their medicine and supplies with them. Some villagers whispered of witchcraft. A few who'd accepted their vaccinations fled to the pagodas, begging for the Buddhist monks' meditations to help retrieve their souls.

Truc knew all of this. His walks through the village at night, the ducks behind him in a row, allowed him to hear much of the gossip and speculation, though he had nothing to say in response. His insomnia allowed him to rest in his room during the day, since his family presumed he was exhausted. Truc preferred this. He didn't know what else to say to his family except that he was sorry.

The orphanage in Saigon was an old French villa surrounded by high salmon-colored walls and a black iron gate that opened into a large courtyard with a broken fountain. It was run by an American organization that could afford to take in what appeared to be hundreds of orphans. Truc was curious if they planned to take all the children to America. He wondered how they could survive there.

Several American workers helped Truc and Phuong carry the makeshift cribs into the house, where others rushed over to coo before taking the infants away to be bathed and fed. In the living room, a Vietnamese worker named Hoa spoke with Phuong concerning the babies' medical histories. Truc sat awkwardly on one of the metal chairs, conscious of the various eyes on him.

Phuong would be staying. She'd help the babies adjust and help monitor their health for a week before returning to the Delta.

How will you get home? Truc asked.

I can take the bus. You've already done so much.

One of the workers carried in a freshly bathed infant, his hair damp and matted against his forehead. It took Truc a moment before realizing it was one of their orphans. He smiled when the infant grabbed for Truc's index finger, his impulsive grip soft and puffy.

Truc declined an invitation to stay for dinner. Their shoes clicked on the empty concrete courtyard. Phuong took Truc's hands in hers, undeterred by his initial instinct to resist, and squeezed them.

I will never forget what you've done.

And I won't forget what you've done. He didn't mean it to sound spiteful. He did not say anything else to fix it, but did not let go of her hands either.

How could you think I didn't know your father died?

I don't know, Truc said.

I did. I had to. I still need to know what happens in your life.

Truc let go of her hands, letting his own fall to his sides.

I wanted to see you after I heard about your father. I almost did. Phuong smiled sadly. Then I prayed that you would come to me.

They stood in silence for a long time. I can pick you up, Truc said. Take you home.

That's all right. I don't know exactly when I can return. The bus will be fine.

Okay. He turned to leave.

Good-bye, Truc.

Good-bye.

It was almost evening, the day's heat rising from the soil, warming the city in place of the departed sun. Traffic back to the Delta would be crowded any way he chose. The ducks chattered noisily in the back of the van, reminding Truc he needed to stop at the open-air market to get rid of them. But on the way, he decided to turn around. Realizing he didn't mind the birds' honking, actually appreciated their company, he decided they would all go home.

VISITORS

A TRUCK RATTLED DOWN Brookhurst Avenue, its trailing gust nearly dragging Bac Nguyen with it. Bac Nguyen's loafers locked into the sidewalk, his hands clasping the grocery bags on each side. A few seconds and he regained balance. The rim of his fedora irritated his forehead with sweat, but Bac Nguyen refused to put down the bags. Food markets in the States used disposable plastic sacks for groceries, instead of the sturdy cardboard boxes provided in Vietnam. The meat and vegetables strained against the flimsy material. Bac Nguyen's knuckles whitened. Despite the dull pain in his joints, he gripped the bags tightly. His family planned to make a special dinner that night for his granddaughter's birthday. Bac Nguyen was in charge of having groceries ready when his daughter and son-in-law returned home from work.

Bac Nguyen squinted in the sun's glare, trying to make out the street name swinging from the stoplight. Bolsa Avenue. He did not remember whether he should turn left or right. His daughter had written him directions that morning before leaving for work, but Bac Nguyen had lost them in the market. He considered both options. On the left was another Vietnamese shopping center. On the right, an automobile dealership. He could not recall seeing the shiny collection of cars before. But then again, the other stores didn't look familiar either.

Bac Nguyen pulled at the sleeves of his jacket. He had dressed too warmly. Bac Nguyen rarely left his daughter's house except on the weekends for Sunday Mass and trips to the Vietnamese shopping mall, and that was with his family. He would always wear one of his suits, either the dark blue or the charcoal gray. Never the black one, which was reserved for special occasions. But Bac Nguyen realized the absurdity of dressing so formally for a simple trip to the supermarket. He understood the instant he stepped through the automatic doors and saw both employees and customers alike in T-shirts and tennis shoes. They must have believed him such a foolish old man, an obvious new refugee. They probably knew this was the first time he had ventured out to Little Saigon alone. He avoided the checker's eyes as she rang up the items at the register, his shame was so great. This wouldn't have happened if his wife were still alive. And now he was hot. Sweat pooled in his armpits, the folds in his elbows, the back of his knees. He would have to ask his daughter to get the suit professionally cleaned.

A police car glided by, and Bac Nguyen lowered his head on instinct. He'd adopted the strategy most other Vietnamese immigrants had regarding police enforcement. Stay out of the way, bow the head in false respect, say nothing. Then they can't trick you into trouble. This policy, while only somewhat effective in Vietnam, worked quite well with the police in the States.

A young, shorthaired Vietnamese boy sat nearby on a bus bench reading a thick book. He wore a long-sleeved shirt and light-colored slacks. Pearls of sweat beaded on his temples. His forehead creased in concentration, and Bac Nguyen hesitated about interrupting him from his studies.

Excuse me, young man, he said, hoping this boy could speak Vietnamese. May I bother you for a minute?

The boy folded a small corner on the page and closed the book. It isn't a bother, Bac, he said, looking up. He had a straight nose, wide, blinking eyes, and a composure similar to Bac Nguyen's wife, a self-possessed poise that only went away with smiling.

Bac Nguyen exhaled in relief and carefully set the groceries onto the hot concrete, propping them next to the bench so they wouldn't spill. I recently moved here and I am having trouble finding my daughter's home. I have the address.

He reached into his pocket for an index card his daughter had given him for such occasions.

The boy nodded in recognition after examining the card. Yes, you're only five blocks that way. He pointed toward the shopping center.

Bac Nguyen took the boy's hand into his when he gave him back the card and squeezed it in gratitude.

I am a forgetful old man.

Not at all. When I arrived last year, it took me weeks to find my way around.

I came over last month, Bac Nguyen said.

The boy nodded. I'm glad to help. Have a nice afternoon, Bac. He opened his book and began reading again.

You too, child. Bac Nguyen felt embarrassed wasting the young man's time in silly conversation. The boy needed to study. Bac Nguyen bent forward to pick up his groceries. He organized them in the sensible arrangement he'd discovered at the grocery store: the three lighter bags on his right hand, the two heavier ones on the left. But as he laced his fingers into the last handle to push up his forearm, the weight of its contents became too great. The plastic ripped, meat and vegetables gushing over into a soggy heap on the sidewalk. One of the ground beef packages punctured on impact, a trickle of blood oozing into a crack in the concrete.

Bac Nguyen fell to his knees, ignoring the sharp pain gripping his legs. His arms scrambled for the runaway cabbage rolling for the gutter. He nearly fell rescuing it, but he had to. He'd spent the leftover money from groceries on an espresso and a Vietnamese newspaper. A little treat he now regretted dearly.

He turned around, clutching the vegetable to his chest, and saw that the boy had left his seat to help retrieve the other spilled items.

Thank you, Bac Nguyen said, his eyes fixed on the cabbage.

Don't worry about it.

Together they tried to place the remaining items into the still-intact grocery bags. Bac Nguyen was momentarily distracted by their shadows on the concrete, their heads nearly touching, the two of them working together. He remembered Anh, and, with only the thought of his youngest son, Bac Nguyen's eyes immediately swelled.

This isn't going to work, the boy said.

Bac Nguyen looked up, blinking away the moisture from his eyes. What do you mean?

These bags are already too full. They'll break if you carry them any farther like this. The boy looked at his watch. He bit his lower lip, like he was considering something. Then he looked at Bac Nguyen.

I can help you take these home, the boy said. Reluctance lingered in his voice, and it made Bac Nguyen feel awful.

But do you have to be somewhere?

My next class is a lecture, so I can get notes from another classmate.

Are you sure? Bac Nguyen didn't want to be any more of a nuisance than he'd already been.

It isn't a problem, Bac, the boy said. He had already begun loading some of the groceries into his gray backpack.

The boy insisted on carrying most of the bags, despite Bac Nguyen's protests. The streets in Little Saigon were near several freeways and often busy with traffic. Bac Nguyen wouldn't admit this out loud, but he felt safer walking with the taller young man. Speeding cars could easily overlook a hunched-over old man, but not this boy who held his head high and spine straight. They walked side by side, the boy slightly ahead with Bac Nguyen doing his best to keep up. Feeling slightly ineffectual with only one bag to hold, Bac Nguyen tried to keep them entertained by asking the boy questions.

Do you live nearby?

A few blocks from Brookhurst.

With your parents?

No, I live with my brothers.

What are you studying in school?

Economics.

A businessman, how wonderful!

Well, not yet.

Nevertheless, that's excellent. Little Saigon needs more businessmen. Economy is the foundation to any strong community.

The boy smiled, Bac Nguyen realized, for the first time since they met. I think so, too.

Your parents must be proud.

The boy's smile faded as quickly as it had appeared. They died, Bac, the boy said, in Vietnam.

Bac Nguyen stopped walking. I'm so sorry.

Thank you.

That must have been terrible, Bac Nguyen said, and to come to a new country. At least you have your brothers.

Yes, I'm very thankful for them.

We've lost so many people. Bac Nguyen placed his arm on the boy's, and they began walking again. My wife and son died during the war, too.

They've taken so much from us, the boy said.

Yes, the Communists were heartless. Bac Nguyen still couldn't control the rush of blood to his head remembering that Communist sniper who gunned Anh down that day so long ago on the beach in Vung Tau.

You misunderstand Bac, the boy said. I wasn't meaning the Communists.

Oh, Bac Nguyen said, slightly confused, I just assumed—

I was talking about the Americans.

They were approaching his daughter's house. At the home across the street, several children in bathing suits were hopping over a water sprinkler to keep cool. Children's bicycles and skateboards occupied most of the block's driveways. Many of the cars were gone, taking their owners away to make money to keep these cramped, identical tract homes.

When his daughter first explained to him the idea of paying a mortgage for a home in the States, Bac Nguyen didn't understand. In Vietnam, before the war had infiltrated the South, the house he owned lay on the land he owned. But here, even if one owned a home, one still had to pay for it every month. Another confusing American custom.

Bac Nguyen was sorry the walk to his daughter's house didn't take longer. This boy was interesting to talk to. Bac Nguyen craved interesting conversations. He never considered himself a talker until his wife died, and he realized how necessary all the everyday things they said to each other were. He missed conversations, any kind. His daughter and son-in-law were often too tired from working all day to really talk, and their children only wanted to scream and play or watch television.

Bac Nguyen fumbled for the key to open the front door. He turned and bowed his head slightly to the boy. You must be thirsty. Come in for some tea.

Thank you, but I really should be leaving.

Please. You've been so generous with your time. Let me thank you. What about some iced lemonade? Bac Nguyen hoped the desperation in his voice wasn't too obvious.

The boy hesitated for a moment, indecision tugging at his mouth, but he finally nodded.

They left their shoes outside the door. Inside, the house smelled of steamed rice, fried eggs, and Chinese sausage, from the family's breakfast that morning. Bac Nguyen led the way past the living room and family room to the kitchen. The boy unloaded his backpack on the counter and Bac Nguyen quickly stuffed the perishable meats and vegetables, plastic bags and all, into the refrigerator.

When he turned back, the boy was shifting on his heels, looking around the house awkwardly. He sympathized with the boy's discomfort. The house was pristinely composed—like a museum—with the complicated, oversized entertainment system in the family room and decorative china and glassware carefully placed on neatly dusted shelves in the living room. While Bac Nguyen always enjoyed a handsome home—his own in Vietnam before the war had been rather large and impressive—he felt a detached coldness in his daughter's house. Perhaps because it was in the States, and everything in it was essentially American. He didn't know. He hoped he would get over the feeling in time and come to see this unfamiliar place as his home.

Please sit down, Bac Nguyen said to the boy, gesturing to the kitchen table. Would you like tea or lemonade?

Tea is fine.

Bac Nguyen checked to make sure there was enough filtered water in the kettle and turned the stove on. He set out the teapot, two cups, and the jasmine tea leaves. At the table, he took his hat off, removed his jacket, and hung it neatly on the back of the chair.

I apologize if I shocked you earlier, the boy said when Bac Nguyen sat down across from him. Perhaps it was inappropriate to say.

No, child, I admire your honesty. He plugged in the small portable fan on the table and closed his eyes as the breeze caressed his perspiring face. There's no need to be sorry.

I should know that opinions differ when it comes to the Americans.

It's a complicated issue.

Not for me. They destroyed our country, then they left. To ease their guilty conscience, they took some of us in. It's really simple.

Bac Nguyen wondered what this young boy knew about the war and the Americans' role, where all this anger came from. He saw it in his own children, the passionate, resolute ideology, the black-and-white view of history. Only with time, experience, and loss could a person realize that there isn't simply one bad guy or one good guy—that in war, there are many sides at fault.

But you're in a better place, child. You have a good life here, Bac Nguyen said. Don't you?

It would have been nice if I had a say in it.

So you would rather be in Vietnam? Living in poverty with nothing to eat?

This government is no better than the one we left behind.

Of course it isn't. I know better than anyone else, child, I was questioned and falsely imprisoned by the Communists several times. But I survived.

The kettle's whistle, which Bac Nguyen hadn't initially heard, escalated into a wail. He walked over to the stove and, with a rag, lifted the kettle handle and poured the steaming liquid into the teapot.

They sipped the tea in silence. Bac Nguyen wanted to say something to end the awkwardness; as the host he should, but the boy seemed to be deep in thought, like he was formulating a response to the last thing Bac Nguyen had said.

Do you ever miss Vietnam?

Of course, Bac Nguyen said. It's my home.

That's how I feel. Even though I don't remember much of it, I still feel like it's my home, and this place, while nice, isn't. It's like I'm visiting, and I've overstayed my welcome. Why are we here when we lost so many people there? Shouldn't we be with them? It seems unfair that while the people we love are rotting in Vietnam, we're here enjoying a better life.

We have to go on, child. While I don't have much longer, you have your whole life. But you do have a point about the people we love.

Really? The boy wore a smile that leaned more toward amused than grateful.

Yes, Bac Nguyen said, struggling to remember his train of thought. It had been a while since he'd proselytized. We spend so much energy and time on the larger issues, religion, country, political parties, that we ignore the smaller ones, like family and our homes, which are ultimately more important. I will always regret every political meeting I went to when my wife begged me to stay home with her. I will always regret every minute I chose not to spend with her because I will never have it back. Do you have a girlfriend?

The boy bit his lip before answering. Yes.

You should concentrate your energies on her. Forget about these politics. They took too much time away from me and my wife.

That won't happen to us.

It might. Listen to my words. I've had much suffering and sorrow in my years.

She will always be the most important thing in my life, the boy said.

Bac Nguyen shook his head. If only the young realized all this confidence they exuded could quickly sour into foolishness. It's easy to believe that, Bac Nguyen said. But you take for granted what is there every day. A free government. A fair government. These unattainable ideals become so much more attractive than the woman you wake up with every day.

Bac Nguyen stood up. Excuse me for a moment.

He walked to his bedroom, the only one on the bottom floor of the house. It was simply furnished with a twin bed, a dresser, and a desk. Bac Nguyen knelt to the carpet and pulled out a wooden box from underneath the bed. He pushed aside the folded bills, both American and Vietnamese currency, to pull out a smaller black marble box. Cradling it close to his chest with both arms, he stood and walked back to the kitchen.

Setting the box on the table, Bac Nguyen paused dramatically before opening it, revealing long glittering rows of necklaces, bracelets, and earrings.

See this? This is all I have of my wife. I used to think her jewelry was the vainest, most frivolous part of her, the only part of her I didn't like. Now I think it's precious. I look at them and remember all of her as beautiful.

There was one gold necklace dangling on the edge, nearly falling. The clasp was loose. Bac Nguyen lifted it out, rubbing the thin chain between his fingers. It sparkled in the faint beam of sunlight streaming through the curtains from the window.

Bac Nguyen looked at the boy. A shadow crossed his solemn face.

How serious are you about this girl?

I'm going to marry her. The jut of his chin, thin lips nearly white pressed together. Like his son Anh when he told Bac Nguyen he was enlisting in the South Vietnamese army. Full of confidence, denial of any fear.

Holding the necklace up to eye level, Bac Nguyen took the boy's hand and pressed his palm open. He let the necklace slowly drop into a loose coil in the boy's hand.

My daughter never wanted her mother's jewelry. It was never her taste, she prefers more Western styles.

After a long moment, the boy closed his mouth, swallowing hard. Are you sure?

It's only one necklace. I have plenty of others to remember her by. Bac Nguyen felt confident for his rather bold generosity. All this beautiful jewelry, wasting away in a box. For one to be shown off again, worn proudly on a young woman's neck as a symbol of this boy's love for her, that seemed appropriate. That seemed right.

The boy had to go. He had a class at five-thirty he couldn't miss.

I hope I didn't take up too much of your time, Bac Nguyen said as he walked the boy to the door.

Not at all. The boy gave a small, polite smile. He looked much younger when he smiled. Thank you.

Bac Nguyen realized something and gave a small laugh. I just realized we didn't introduce ourselves formally. How silly. He held out his hand. My name is Bac Nguyen.

Vinh, the boy said, taking his hand. His grip on Bac Nguyen tightened slightly.

Nice to meet you, Vinh. Bac Nguyen squeezed his hand back. Your parents would have been proud of you.

As the boy walked away, a fuzziness settled into Bac Nguyen's head. The last time he remembered this sensation was when Anh left for the army. Bac Nguyen couldn't admit to himself, as he shook his son's hand for the last time, that he knew Anh was going to die. He certainly hoped that wasn't the same fate for this boy Vinh. Perhaps it was only loss, simple as that.

Where the hell have you been?

Vinh pushed past Chau, one of the younger brothers, to get to the refrigerator. All that jasmine tea had made him thirsty for something cold, really cold.

I said, where you been? Chau asked. Hung's looking for you.

I was scouting, he knew that, Vinh said, finding the last beer in the back. He'd have to remind one of the roosters to go out and get some more.

Well, what took you so long?

Vinh turned and shut the refrigerator with the heel of his

foot. He popped off the bottle cap while surveying the apartment. The stereo's bass was turned up to the maximum, so he could feel the rhythmic thumping through his sneakers. In the living room, several of the boys lay transfixed by their video game, blue light illuminating their wide eyes and open mouths, sounds of electronic gunfire occasionally bursting through the bass. Lights turned on in both of the bedrooms down the hall. The lease stipulated only four people could live in the apartment, but some of the other brothers had been kicked out of their parents' houses and were crashing there until they could find their own place. That was a while ago. Vinh bet they weren't even looking yet.

What do you think took me so long? Vinh asked.

The boy's face split into a grin. You found one?

Vinh nodded, tipping the bottle back and taking in a long drink.

All right! Chau's youth betrayed him as he slapped the kitchen counter with satisfaction. He still got a thrill out of home invasions, Vinh realized, still found them fun.

Hung sauntered in sleepily, a freshly lit cigarette in hand. He leaned his hip against the wall for support. Got one?

Yeah, Vinh said, it's over near Newman. It was a grandpa. The boys from the living room had wandered over to stand behind Hung, looking at Vinh intently.

Did you just tail him, or did you get him to talk to you? Hung asked.

I was only gonna tail him, but then the old man spilled his groceries. Helped him carry them home.

Hung smiled. What a Boy Scout.

Vinh struggled to continue. No security system. There's a big-screen, CD player and VCR, some nice china, jewelry—

He stopped abruptly, putting his hand on the kitchen counter. The beer tasted skunked. Vinh felt nauseous, a sour bile on the roof of his mouth.

We'll go tonight, Hung said.

No, Vinh said before he could catch himself. The boys stared at him. Hung was Vinh's old foster brother, the one who brought him into 354. Vinh never disagreed with Hung in front of the other boys and hardly ever in private.

Why not? Hung asked.

Vinh could hear his heartbeat over the stereo bass. They'll be home tonight, Vinh said slowly, hoping it came out casual. The grandpa had groceries for a big dinner.

Hung shook his head. We gotta do it tonight.

Why? Another mistake. Vinh was never one to question Hung.

You know why, Hung said impatiently.

Vinh suddenly remembered. They had debts to pay. A couple of months' rent, utility bills, and the most urgent, an IOU that, while the sum was unclear, Vinh suspected was up in the thousands. Hung's gambling debt. If one brother was in trouble, they all helped out. That was why Vinh had gone scouting for a family to rob that day. They couldn't afford to get behind on any debts. Wimp. Vinh had never hesitated on a home invasion before. He couldn't understand why he was stalling on this one. Senile old man. Why couldn't he just shut up? Why did he have to talk so long, wasting Vinh's time? And why did he stay to listen?

While Hung gave each boy his assignment, Vinh stayed quiet, writing up directions to the target for each car. But he kept getting distracted by Hung's hand gestures, which seemed to grow bigger and more dramatic with each minute that passed. He looked like a politician. Vinh had never noticed it before, usually so caught up in what Hung was saying.

Since they'd broken up, Kim had become a lot more honest about her feelings about Vinh's brothers, how much she despised them all. Vinh didn't believe half the things she said, knew she couldn't really think that way of the boys who'd supported her for so long. The most disturbing insult, though, was about Hung, maybe because it was so surprising. Kim had grown up with Hung, too. He'd been an older brother to both of them in the foster homes.

He's just a punk, Kim had said. He thinks he's smart because he's leading 354, but he's not. And you guys follow him around like he's some kind of prophet, which isn't saying much for you either.

What did she know. Vinh tried to concentrate on his penmanship, which was often illegible. He pressed hard on the ballpoint pen, making each letter large and dark. Kim was just jealous. She thought he'd chosen his brothers over her because he refused to leave them. She was applying for some secretarial job and thought she was now above them. Vinh knew better. Kim would be back, eventually, when she realized selling out to the Americans wasn't worth it.

Look what happened to those who did. The orphans adopted by American families didn't even think they were Vietnamese anymore. And those who were left behind, unwanted, forgotten, had to suffer in foster homes. For a long time Vinh was angry about it, but now he realized they were better off. They knew where they stood with the Americans. The golden children didn't. Kim would come around, just like she had before. He only had to be patient.

Vinh rode shotgun in the first car out since he'd scouted.

When the address was confirmed, they waited until all the lights went out, not only in the target, but every other house on the block. Once that happened, Chau and Kha paged the other boys to head over.

Vinh shifted in his seat, unable to get comfortable. I'm cold, he said.

Well, you should have brought your jacket, Hung said from the driver's seat. We're not turning the car on.

Just for a minute, I'm freezing.

Someone could hear, you know that.

Light a cigarette, Chau said.

Fuck off, Vinh said.

What's his problem? Chau kicked the back of Vinh's seat. Hard. What's your problem?

Leave him alone, Hung said. Then he looked over to Vinh. Kim still ducking your calls?

She was, but that wasn't what he was thinking about. Vinh turned his head to look out the window. The old man's house was virginal, no complicated locks or alarm systems that Vinh could detect. This would be an easy job, in and out, unless the old man or any of his family started making noise. He really hoped they wouldn't make any noise.

The others are here, Kha said. Vinh looked up. Sure enough, two cars with their lights off were coasting in neutral down the block. Vinh watched as one of the cars stopped in front of the target to let Vu out, so he could smash out the telephone box on the side of the house. They always put Vu in charge of cutting off the phone lines, though at fifteen he was still a rooster, not an official member of the gang. But he was almost there. Vu could bust a line with a hammer in under a minute, quieter and faster than any of them.

Vinh sat forward suddenly. Wait.

What? Hung asked.

Stop Vu.

Why? Everyone in the car sat up in full alert.

It's too fast. We're still early.

Are you kidding? Kha said. We've been waiting here for over two hours.

I said it's too soon. They might still be awake.

So they might be, so what? There was an ugly sneer on Hung's face. What the hell is the matter with you, Vinh? You been acting like this all night.

He never should have told the old man his name. Vinh felt so stupid. That was a wannabe's mistake, not someone who'd been doing this for four years. The old man was so damn sweet, throwing Vinh off guard with the necklace, that he had let himself get weak. No one in 354 could know about this fuckup. Hung would kill him.

One of the cars turned to park at the end of the block and flashed its lights once to signal they were ready for lookout.

Let's go.

They were behind him because he was supposed to lead, but he felt their breaths and steps too close, like they were pushing him forward. Their shadows from the streetlamps bobbed across the concrete. They always wore black for jobs, convenient because most of their clothes were that color anyway, but tonight the shade seemed darker, more sinister than usual. Some of them had already pulled panty hose over their faces. Someone tossed one over Vinh's shoulder, and he yanked it on automatically, the constraint of breathing suddenly a comfort to him. At least he was feeling something familiar, real.

Hung stepped ahead of him and quietly jammed the front lock open with a filed-down car key. They stepped inside the home, cool air welcoming their faces, courtesy of central air-conditioning. Several boys headed to the family room to dismantle the entertainment system. Others went to search for a separate office or den where computer equipment would be kept. Vinh had already arranged to go for the centerpiece, the old man's bedroom, where the family cash was likely kept.

A light turned on upstairs. Shouting. Must have been the old man's daughter and son-in-law. Problem was no one was shutting them up.

Shit, Hung muttered. Goddamn roosters.

Vinh and Hung hurried upstairs and turned into the first door, the main bedroom. At the foot of the bed, Vu and another newbie, Khanh, were taking turns kicking the son-in-law in the stomach as he writhed on the floor. Behind them, the daughter was beating the phone on the nightstand, screaming at it to work.

Hung smoothly grabbed the woman by the hair and pressed her head to the floor. He leaned his lips to her ear and whispered something, probably advising her to stay quiet or he'd shoot her. Vinh grabbed the phone and jerked the cord out of the wall socket. While Hung crossed her hands behind her back, Vinh laced the cord around the woman's wrists, tying it several times.

After the woman was subdued, Hung tossed a roll of duct tape to the roosters to tie up the son-in-law, who now lay slumped over in the corner of the bedroom. Blood smeared along the wall from where he fell over.

You little fucks, Hung said to the boys, as he and Vinh stepped out to check the rest of the upstairs. We don't have time for this.

They should have pretended to be asleep. They should have

known about home invasions. The roosters were just supposed to tie them up and scare them a little. Enough so they won't think about calling the police afterward, though they probably wouldn't anyway. That's why Vietnamese gangs robbed their own people. Gangs knew their people wouldn't trust the police to protect them. Police in Vietnam were a step below street merchants, they were so corrupt. They had no reason to believe the Americans, who couldn't understand their accents anyway, would be any better.

Down the hall, two more bedrooms, the kids' rooms. One was empty and in the other, two little girls curled together under the covers, their eyes full of tears. The bed was shaking, the headboard tapping against the wall.

Hung grabbed the bedspread and snatched it off. The kids' legs were tangled together. One of the girls had wet herself, a large dark stain spreading across the sheet.

Vinh walked over to the closet door and opened it. Get in. When they didn't move, he pulled the knife from his back pocket and flipped it open, holding it up to the light so they could see it clearly. Get in now.

They screamed and nearly tripped over each other rushing to get inside the closet. Vinh grabbed the desk chair in the corner and propped it beneath the knob. He kicked the chair several times to make sure it wouldn't come loose.

When they returned downstairs, the others were almost done. Speakers, a television, CD player, carried away so dutifully in a row, like ants at a picnic. The family room looked stripped down on one side without the entertainment system. Cobwebs and dust draped the now naked wall.

Vinh wandered from room to room with a strange sense of satisfaction, which he welcomed. Sometimes in looking at the chaos, the overturned cabinets and drawers, the broken dishes and spilled papers, Vinh convinced himself that they were ultimately doing these people a favor. All of them in such a delusion about attaining this material dream of fortune and comfort, but at what expense? Didn't they realize they'd always be under the thumb of this government? It wasn't any better than Vietnam just because this government was more successful at deluding their people. They were fools to believe they could actually live among the Americans and become one of them. They never would. They would never be allowed.

What are you doing?

Vinh turned.

Hung glared at him from behind a large porcelain vase he was hugging with both arms. Will you get Grandpa already? We gotta get out of here.

His bedroom door was closed. Vinh pressed his hand on the knob and eased it open. The old man must have been hard of hearing to sleep through all this. Vinh stepped in quietly. No need to wake the old man. Just get the box and go.

The old man snored softly like a child. Vinh quickly checked for valuables in the open, but quickly surmised that, as with most old people, the true treasures were stashed under the bed. Vinh knelt to the floor, trying to ignore the rise and fall of the blankets with the old man's breaths, and felt around. There was a lot of crap to sort through, newspapers, magazines, records, all kinds of junk. Finally, he pulled out a wooden box, lifted the lid, and there it was. He quickly deposited all the bills into the small bag tucked in his belt. At least several thousand. Not bad. Another Vietnamese superstition to count on: not only did they distrust the police, but banks as well, preferring to hoard the cash in their homes, most often with the oldest members of the family. Vinh couldn't understand why they didn't see the impracticality of this. Grandpas and grannies can't be expected to defend the family treasures.

As he pushed the box back under the bed, Vinh looked over to make sure the old man was still sleeping. He was. On his bedside table next to him was an eight-by-ten black-and-white of an old woman, the wife. Vinh guessed it was positioned like that so whenever the old man woke up and turned to his side she would be the first thing he saw. Pathetic. But it also made him think about Kim, though he hoped she wouldn't get as fat and ugly as the old man's wife did. Though she was being difficult right now, Vinh still knew he wanted to be with Kim forever.

They were never into that mushy stuff that other couples fell for. It was deeper than that. But maybe because he never did the flowers and chocolate crap, she thought they weren't real. Maybe he'd have to do a little of that to show that he did love her. The old man was right, though he yacked on for quite a while, it was the love, it was the connection that was worth more than wasting your life away for the community. He needed to show Kim she meant more to him than the boys. The necklace was a good first step. But any guy could give a girl one necklace. Vinh could do more than that.

He pulled the larger box back out and located the marble jewelry box. This jewelry had to be old. Handcrafted, class, tradition, elegance. You couldn't buy this for cheap in the States. Kim was worth it. She deserved all this and when he gave it to her, she'd understand.

He tucked the box under his arm, stood up, and walked softly toward the door. Vinh didn't figure that one of the boys would turn the hallway light on, but when he opened the door, a shaft of light came streaming through, right onto the old man's face.

Let's go, Vinh said to the others, pulling the door shut behind him. He felt the door tug back, the knob jiggling. The old man was awake, standing right behind it..

What's happening? Who is there?

Everyone was getting out. Vinh was supposed to be the last one. He held on to the door, until almost everyone was gone. He finally let go, hoping the old man would fall after pulling on it so hard. Vinh ran down the hall past the living room and family room, now stripped barren, tripping over several overturned chairs and tables until he reached the front door.

He felt a hand on his shoulder and he spun around, yanking it away. Get off, old man.

What are you doing, child? He looked even sadder in his wrinkled, worn pajamas, the sleep crusted in his swollen, blinking eyes. That's mine.

He reached for his jewelry box with shaking, liver-spotted hands. Instinctively, Vinh brought his arms up, smacking the old man's face hard with the jewelry box. He thought he could hear the man's jaw crack. The old man staggered back, his hands flying to his mouth, blood streaming between his fingers.

Vinh turned and ran. They were waiting for him in front, engine running, the passenger door wide-open.

C'mon, Vinh, Chau yelled. Move it!

Vinh? Vinh, child, is that you?

The voice was soft and frail, but in the cold night air, soared furiously through Vinh's ears, down his throat, nearly strangling his heart.

Vinh froze, stunned. The boys had heard it, too. They stared at Vinh in horror, disbelief, betrayal.

Slowly turning around, Vinh watched the old man stagger

toward him, blood trailing down his chin, his arms outstretched like he wanted to embrace.

Vinh? Why are you doing this? What would your parents say?

When he was within arm's length, Vinh reached up and smacked him again with the jewelry box, this time clear across the forehead.

The old man snapped back onto the lawn, then curled into the fetal position, rolling in pain. Vinh walked over until he was right above him, lifted his foot, and brought it down onto the old man's face. Once. Twice. Vinh stepped away, trying hard to catch his breath, then proceeded to kick the old man in the stomach, then along his back, his legs, anywhere he could.

You don't know my name. Kick. You don't know anything about me.

Someone grabbed him from behind roughly, fists full of his T-shirt. For a moment he was afraid it was the cops, but it was Chau. His nails dug into Vinh's back.

Let's go, man, let's go.

They pushed him into the backseat. Hung put the car in drive and slammed on the gas before they could even get the door closed.

The car was silent, except for the heavy breathing of adrenaline aftermath. Vinh lay slumped in the backseat, holding on to the jewelry box as tightly as he could.

At the first red light, Hung couldn't restrain himself any longer and reached over the driver's seat to smack Vinh across the face twice. Kha finally had to hold him back.

You idiot. Hung glared at him with absolute disgust. What the hell did you do to us?

The light turned green. Chau, who was sitting next to Vinh, wouldn't even look at him.

The jewelry box was slick around the edges, Vinh realized, with the old man's blood. He opened the box carefully and the gold and jewels blinked at him in the light of the streetlamps. Precious. Beautiful.

GATES

OF

SAIGON

THEY KNEW BETTER THAN to move off the buckets, though occasional sighs and slight fidgeting exposed their discomfort. Naked babies filled the room, indistinguishable with their shaved fuzzy hair, listless eyes, and thin limbs spindling over scratched-up pails. Every morning they gathered in the room for toilet training, squatting for several hours until the nuns said they could get up.

Hoa had been told long ago about the necessity of this activity. The nursery was notoriously overcrowded, located in one of the poorest sections of Saigon, and this was the only practical method to potty train so many children. Still, Hoa remembered her sons at this age, crawling on the floor, suckling her breast. They were never forced to hunch over a pail. Hoa didn't even need to glance over at the new American, Steven, to be assured that he was horrified.

Hoa's gaze skimmed over the tops of their heads. Which ones? she asked.

The nun pointed to a particularly emaciated child in the corner, looking like she might slip off her pail at any moment.

Then another finger at a boy who nearly disappeared in his pot. Both children already betrayed signs of their mixed racial heritage, more so, Hoa realized with closer scrutiny, than the others.

In the driveway, Hoa and Steven exchanged several boxes of diapers and baby formula for the two infants, which the nuns pressed to their chests with bows and murmurs of thanks. They peered into the empty car hopefully, but Hoa shook her head. They had other nurseries to get to, a maximum of two per stop. She'd learned a long time ago the problem of succumbing at the first orphanage, though the urge to gather as many babies in her arms as possible never fully went away. The grief now stained Steven's face, his reluctance to leave any children behind when he knew their own facilities were so much better.

After securing the babies in their carriers, they stood aside while the sisters made their tearful good-byes. This sometimes took a while. Hoa supposed it could be worse; at least these women still cared about their charges. A common, lingering result of working in an orphanage was a numbing indifference to the disease and death that crept around the children.

Hoa checked the infants' temperatures. Two fingers on their necks, then across the foreheads. There were many disparities between children in these orphanages and the lucky ones Hoa cared for in Saigon. What she noticed first was skin. Healthy infants bore complexions soft as overripe mangoes. These babies were sucked dry, rib cages and joints sharply visible, their wrinkled bodies so starved for nutrition they fed off themselves. Steven padded them with extra blankets to cushion the blow, should their delicate frames bump against their carriers.

Once seated in the car, Hoa examined the new American's gray complexion and shallow breathing.

Are you feeling all right?

The man nodded slightly and turned to Hoa. How many more stops?

Three. It will be another hour. Hoa looked at her wristwatch. Do you want me to take you back?

Steven shook his head. His thick red hair, which had looked so large that morning at the airport, now clung to his head in limp, wet curls.

Hoa ran the engine until it caught. She would not press the issue again, unless the American complained of stomach pains or began throwing up. These new volunteers were always impatient to do so much their first week, brushing off suggestions to allow time for adjustment to the country's climate and the time change. Their ignorance irritated Hoa, their denial that they could be more in the way than helpful.

The narrow, jammed streets in downtown Saigon required frequent braking, quick acceleration, and focus, especially when street vendors, motorbikes, or other cars strayed too close, which they always did. Hoa's husband had taught her to drive when she was pregnant with their second child. She always remembered with comfort his one hand over her large belly and the other helping her to steer. Throughout her apprehension, he assured her that if she learned to drive correctly, she'd always be safe. Hoa understood that near collisions occurred too often to take notice, unless you were a foreigner. So she patiently ignored Steven's sharp intakes of breath, his instinct to cover his head or shield his eyes each time.

Patriotic mandolin music strummed through the crackling static of the city's rusted loudspeakers that loomed over every street corner. Occasionally, government officials announced news of the war's progress, encouraging, sometimes demanding, loyalty to the state.

After ten minutes, the street pavement evened out, crossing districts, smoothing the drive. The lack of potholes and bumps calmed the American, eventually encouraging him to roll down the window for fresh air. Steven craned his neck out the window as they turned into the new district, his curiosity about the country renewed.

At the end of the street, a golden pagoda stood prominently on a stone-floor plaza, where a woman in white worshiped. When they drove by, they could see that her long dress and pants were soiled with mud and sweat stains. She ignored them, her swollen eyes unblinking, focused on her task of hanging red envelopes on the incense burners.

Where are we now? he asked.

Hoa swerved to avoid a cyclo that was about to cut them off. This is Quan Three. We are near my family's house.

Oh. Steven bent his head to study the map of Saigon that was included in his orientation packet. You grew up here?

No. My hometown is Nha Trang.

He nodded, though he probably didn't know where Nha Trang was, or how beautiful its clean, bare beaches once were, scattered with pickup soccer games and fishermen sorting out the morning catch. But that was so long ago. Even Hoa could not recall the serene details the place once held for her. She would try, especially when her husband Lum was away on duty, but she'd given up, realizing any effort only left her feeling more homesick and alone. Her parents and Lum's parents still lived there, but since Hoa started working, she had little chance to take the children there to visit.

When did you move to Saigon? Steven asked.

After my first son's birth . . . about twenty years ago.

Do you like living in the city?

It is safer here for my boys. I like that.

How did you learn to speak English so well?

I went to French school. My teachers said I had twitchy ears, good for learning languages.

Have you worked at the orphanage long?

About three years ago. The army cannot pay my husband and son very much.

Are they away at battle?

This is a war.

You must miss them so much. Do you worry about them?

Could you check on the babies? Hoa asked, looking in the finger-smudged rearview mirror. They have been so quiet.

Oh, sure, Steven said. He tried to smile before leaving his seat, but his flushed complexion revealed his embarrassment, a realization that his questions had become too personal.

She concentrated on street signs, many of them hard to read. Hoa had worked with enough Americans to understand their need to converse all the time. At first she found their chatty dispositions intrusive, but eventually understood that their curiosity indicated a genuine concern. She tried to remember this with Steven, because of all the Americans entering her country, his intentions, like those of many of the center volunteers, were unselfish.

For years, she reluctantly observed the American army insinuate themselves in her country, realizing the government needed foreign aid, but disliking the swagger and arrogance brought with it. Many of her husband's visits home were spent complaining about the American officers' lack of respect; ordering his men around, undermining Lum's authority and treating him like a low-ranking soldier. And then, after the American president's announcement on television, they changed their minds. Once everywhere on the streets of Saigon, they shrank to only a handful on the streets, mostly guards of the U.S. embassy, so that Hoa actually began to miss them. With their weapons, they'd also taken away their bravado and unwavering confidence that South Vietnam would not fall to the Communists.

The South Vietnamese soldiers were stretched thin. Lum and Tan left for months at a time, visits home suspended for most regiments. Hoa depended on hastily scrawled letters for assurance, and though relieved with each one, she knew they were written critical days before receiving them. On the radio, the South Vietnamese government tried to spin defeats as strategic moves for ultimate victory, but Hoa detected the worry in their voices. Her younger sons observed her compulsively to understand how they should feel about their father's and brother's absence. Hoa held them close to her when they slept, whispering fiercely in their ears of how lucky they were not to be among the orphans she worked with. They had a family. She tried to follow this advice as much as she could.

The next orphanage breezed past her side window, forcing Hoa to jerk her head back and brake suddenly. After looking around to make sure Steven and the babies were fine, Hoa put the car into reverse. Angry drivers leaned on their horns, screaming obscenities from their windows. Hoa calmly ignored them as she slowly backed up and turned onto the correct street.

A game of tag dispersed quickly once the children recognized the van pulling up the driveway. Several staff members emerged from the building, calling out warnings to the older children running toward the car. Although a weekly occurrence, the arrival of new orphans was something everyone paid attention to. For the children, the possibility of new playmates. For the staff, the logistics of where to put them in the already crowded facilities.

The American orphanage was located in a converted villa near a business area of Quan One. The house's two levels contained rooms large enough to accommodate up to ten children each, with the sunroom and veranda upstairs serving as a giant nursery.

The children had the courtyard and two playrooms inside to run around. There had been suggestions to clean out and refill the rotted swimming pool in the backyard, especially in the summer months, but some were afraid of the younger children falling in. Instead, the cooks used the deck to set up an outdoor kitchen for stir-frying and a small garden to grow cilantro and mint leaves.

Steven waved for Bridget, the staff physician, to come over and look at the month-old baby girl they picked up from the last orphanage. Along with general malnutrition and anemia, her breathing indicated respiratory problems. Bridget carried the infant to the house, with Steven following behind.

While the rest of the staff cooed over the new arrivals, Hoa turned to the older children crowding around her. They grinned at her with green lips and teeth. Every month or so, the American embassy sent over boxes of ice-cream treats for the children, injecting a usually sleepy afternoon intended for naps into a sugar rush of hyperactivity.

Did you spoil your appetites? Hoa asked, rubbing one of the boys' protruding belly until he giggled and twisted away from her. You still have to finish your suppers tonight. I don't want to hear any complaints of being too full.

I'm still hungry, a little boy named Duc announced.

Good, Hoa said.

Where are your boys? asked Mui, a young girl originally from Da Lat.

They're at home with their grandparents.

Can you bring them here tomorrow to play with us?

Not tomorrow. They're in school. Maybe next week.

The children gathered in the dining room for dinner, their high, cheerful voices stretching along the walls of the large house. Hoa walked up to the nursery, where Bridget and Steven stood hunched over a crib. The little girl was hooked up to an IV, lying in an incubator. Bridget held a stethoscope to the infant's back, while Steven carefully washed her arms and legs with a damp cloth.

She seems better, Steven said, but Bridget's resigned expression confirmed Hoa's suspicions.

You've been up all day, Hoa said, putting a hand on Steven's shoulder.

I'm fine. I can stay up with the baby.

Hoa and Bridget did not bother to argue with him. Steven believed he'd rescued this child, and her life was his responsibility. They knew how it felt. He would not leave her.

In the director's office downstairs, they gathered for the daily meeting, when staff changed from day to evening shifts. Employees didn't stray far from work during their off-hours. The Americans resided in the villa's guesthouse, while Hoa and the other Vietnamese staff lived nearby with their families. But even they occasionally spent the night on one of the extra cots in the nursery if they stayed at the center late and missed the citywide curfew.

The office was cramped with overstuffed filing cabinets and paper-cluttered tables, with a wall-length window looking out to the empty pool. An old ceiling fan circulated hot, stale air in the room. Staff members sat on foldout chairs or leaned against the wall, while the director, Sophie, sat behind a large metal desk. Thanh, Hoa's closest friend at the center, waved her over to share her seat.

Usually Sophie went over old business concerning their daily tasks. Most of the American volunteers, as former nurses and social workers, remained at the center caring for the children. The Vietnamese employees served as translators either at the center, for infant and supply pickups, or dealings with government ministries. The daily meetings also allowed colleagues to catch up with one another and share anecdotes about the children.

Kissing Thanh's forehead warmly, Hoa playfully squeezed the nape of her neck. Her friend had recently switched over to the night shift, so they rarely worked together anymore.

Thanh's face was pale when Hoa pulled away to look at her. She grasped Hoa's hand urgently. You haven't heard, she said.

Hoa felt her body tense immediately. She thought only of Lum and Tan. Tell me.

The president surrendered the Central Highlands this afternoon.

Hoa looked to the floor, the black grout blurring into the clay red tiles. How many casualties?

It was a bloodless surrender. The North was advancing, so Nguyen van Thieu told our men to withdraw.

Hoa's face grew hot. While relieved it wasn't news of Lum's and Tan's deaths, this was by no means any better. She shouldn't have been surprised, but the shock scraped along her skin, leaving her cold. Their government was giving up. So many battles lost and promises of reversal and now it might all be over.

Let's get started, everyone.

Private conversations fell away when Sophie sat at the table.

A former army nurse, Sophie was a tall, thin woman with curly gray hair she kept in a bun atop her head. She was known to bark at the children if they got too rambunctious, and though they would laugh at her growling, deep voice, they always obeyed her.

Sophie rubbed her eyes tiredly and rested her chin in her hands. You must have all heard by now.

No one responded. Seventeen full-time employees, and no one could come up with anything to say. Their faces, Hoa realized gazing around the room, many young, barely into their twenties or thirties, appeared helpless, confused. The Americans, especially, stared at Sophie, hoping to take a cue from her on how to react.

This clearly makes our jobs much harder, Sophie said. We don't know how much time we have, so we have to consider every case urgent.

Isn't that what we're doing? asked Dang, a young Vietnamese man who supervised the house maintenance.

Before, we operated on little time, Sophie said. Now we know it's really here. Her eyes swept the room, settling briefly, but determinedly, on each staff member. Starting tomorrow, everyone will work an extra half shift. Someone will be assigned to the ministries all day to try and get passports and exit visas. We'll have to irritate them into submission.

Immigration has to be swamped now, Bridget said. Everyone must be trying to get out.

Thanh elbowed Hoa in the side, and they looked at each other. They always knew their jobs were not permanent; the center's function was only to speed along the children's exit from the country. But they weren't expecting this goal to be completed all at once and so soon. Now, Hoa realized, once the children were evacuated, the American staff would go too.

Hoa hooked a finger under the metal seat of her chair and calculated that it had been three weeks since she'd heard from Lum and Tan. She scornfully recalled her son's enthusiasm to enlist after his seventeenth birthday, Lum's encouragement for him to do so, and during their visits home, their descriptions of what they heard enemy prison camps were like. Their faith in the South Vietnamese government, so admirable in its idealism, would turn against them if the Communists claimed victory.

Her thoughts wrapped tightly around this as the meeting continued, the voices buzzing in the background.

We're hiring two additional guards for the center and reactivating the west gate.

Isn't it still broken?

We're getting it fixed tomorrow morning. Dang, could you get on that?

Aren't we overreacting? The city hasn't surrendered.

It's still not safe. The American news radio is anticipating a panic. We need to keep the children protected.

Why can't we just leave now?

We still need paperwork for the babies. If they don't have both a passport and exit visa, they can't leave. Right now only half the children even have a passport.

The children they were specifically talking about were the forty who had adoptive parents waiting for them in America and Canada. But there were more than a hundred or so that didn't have families to go to. These kids tended to be older, closer in age to Hoa's sons. Even if they were evacuated to America, that didn't guarantee them a family. They'd still be orphans, but worse, in a foreign country.

The meeting ended with assignments for extra shifts. Hoa received two evening shifts, which meant overnighters, since they ended after curfew. As everyone left the office, Hoa stayed behind, quietly observing Sophie sort through some paperwork on her desk.

What will happen to the other children? Hoa asked, when Sophie finally looked up.

I'm not sure yet, Sophie said tiredly, setting the folders down. This is all happening so fast. I do understand your concern. I assure you, hon, they won't be forgotten.

So you're taking them, too? Or will you keep the center opened?

I don't know. Sophie avoided her gaze. We don't know anything right now. If we can't care for them, we'll make sure they will be somewhere else.

But there wasn't anywhere else, and Sophie knew that better than anybody. Sophie's center was one of the best orphanage facilities in Saigon. Others with comparable resources were also run by international adoption agencies, and their futures in Vietnam would be endangered if the Communists seized Saigon.

We've received terrible news today, Sophie said, putting an arm around Hoa. But we're going to figure it out, I know we will. She looked at Hoa sympathetically. Oh, hon. Have you heard from your husband and son?

Hoa shook her head. No. I have not been home yet.

Well, for heaven's sakes, go home. Your shift is over, and you look exhausted.

Steven, Hoa said, running a hand through her hair, remembering. I need to give you a report on his training today.

He's getting along, right?

Hoa nodded. Several more weeks, and he should be adjusted.

Sophie waved her hand. That's fine. We might not even be here that long.

When Hoa climbed upstairs to say good-bye to Steven, she found him rocking the baby to his chest. He'd removed the IV from her arm. The baby's eyes were half-open, and her body was still.

She didn't even last an hour, Steven said. His cheeks were shiny with tears. His embrace on the child was fierce.

She was very sick, Hoa said. She put a hand on Steven's arm, but his grip on the little girl only tightened. Any harder, and he was going to bruise the child's skin.

This isn't why I came here, Steven said. I wanted to help.

You are, Hoa said. This does not mean you are not helping. These children are very sick. Some of them will die.

But we were giving her fluids. Bridget prescribed her medicine.

It was too late. This is no one's fault.

Steven shook his head. We need to get them out of here. This place will kill them.

He was grieving. He was in shock. It was not the time for Hoa to tell him that the place he regarded as death was what she still considered home. Instead, she patiently crouched beside him, waiting. The first casualty was always devastating. Nearly half an hour passed before his grasp finally slackened. After carefully extricating the child from his arms, Hoa carried the baby and deposited her to the staff nurse on duty.

From the veranda, Hoa could see the older children wandering the courtyard, searching the bushes and grass for frogs and lizards to play with, their foreheads dimpled in concentration. The curfew siren swelled through the air, temporarily unsettling the nursery. Hoa quickly closed the glass doors, and the babies returned to slumber. Turning around, Hoa stared at the clock above the doors resignedly. She'd have to wait to return home until the next day.

Her sons' rosy cheeks stuck to the damp cotton sheet, their knees curled up to their chins. Through the gauzy mosquito netting, their bodies appeared fuzzy and delicate. Though exhausted, Hoa chose to sit on the chair by the door and watch them. It was after dawn, and outside, the crickets chirped like it was still nighttime.

She did not mind that her three sons seemed impervious to her genes, miniature offshoots of her husband. They had Lum's crescent-shaped eyes that always appeared pleased and amused with the world. This sometimes made it difficult to speak to her sons seriously, especially when she had to scold them, because while their heads would bob obediently, those laughing eyes revealed rebellious natures. Most of the time she was proud of her boys' adventurous spirits. But with the war, it had become another vulnerability. She hated leaving them at home while she was at work.

Unable to resist any longer, Hoa kicked off her shoes, parted the netting, and crawled into bed. She soundly kissed each boy on the forehead, stirring them awake.

Mother, you're tickling me, the younger boy, Cung, laughed. He playfully grabbed her arm and nuzzled against her waist. Mmmm, you smell like fish.

Where were you, Mother? the older boy, Van, asked, yawning.

I was at work, child. Have you been good for Ba Minh?

She wouldn't let us outside even once yesterday. Van poked his head under Hoa's elbow and rested his cheek on her shoulder. We could only play in the courtyard.

Did you obey her?

He hesitated a second too long. Yes.

You must obey her, Hoa said sternly. It's very dangerous to be out on the streets by yourselves right now.

Why? Cung asked, sitting up to scratch his stomach. Did the war come?

No, Hoa said. The war is not here. We are safe.

But I heard the Viet Cong are coming soon, Van said. Is that true?

Who told you that?

I heard someone tell Ba Minh yesterday. Now all she does is listen to the radio, but she won't let us listen with her.

No one is coming. But you must obey her. The war isn't here, but it is close by, and I don't want anything bad to happen to my boys.

The war won't come, will it? Cung asked. Father and Tan said they wouldn't let that happen.

They're going to try their best.

After the boys drifted back to sleep, Hoa slipped out of bed. She closed their bedroom door behind her and walked outside to the kitchen. Her bare feet chilled on the frigid tiled floor. The widow would be up soon, and she wanted to prepare breakfast before she could say anything to her about the night before.

Hoa and her family had moved to this house several years ago, located in a wealthy neighborhood they normally couldn't afford. Her landlady, a widow with no children, had owned a fabric store that burned down several years ago, leaving her with little savings. Her house, a spacious one-floor with a central courtyard for a cherry tree garden, had been in her family for generations, and to keep it, she rented out two bedrooms to Hoa's family. For additional money, Ba Minh also watched the boys during the day, but disliked it when Hoa didn't return on schedule, especially since she openly disapproved of her tenant's job.

On the way home, Hoa stopped at the open-air market as the vendors were setting up and bought some fresh eggs, baguettes, and a small watermelon. She couldn't ignore the fact that the city's atmosphere had changed. Fewer children played in the streets. Cyclists peered suspiciously from under their conical hats at anything that passed. There was no carefree gossiping. The vendors at the market mumbled their prices.

In the kitchen, Hoa gathered the necessities to prepare Ba Minh's favorite breakfast. She arranged the baguettes on a tray and set it in the oven. She lit the red clay stove and placed a small pan over it.

Ba Minh soon emerged from the master bedroom, roused with the smells of crackling oil and toasting French bread. Nearly seventy years old, the widow had aged remarkably well, with few white hairs in her black bun, hardly any olive spots on her smooth face, and only faint wrinkles around her eyes. Good morning, she said, shuffling over in her red nylon slippers to stand with Hoa over the stove.

Did you rest well? Hoa asked.

I did, but I know you didn't. She rubbed Hoa's arm soothingly. Those Americans work you too hard.

It was my fault. I was helping one of the new volunteers, and I missed curfew. Hoa neatly cracked the egg in half and dropped it on the sizzling pan.

We were worried, she said, taking the broken shell from Hoa. Especially after yesterday's news. Terrible. Bac Do passed the American embassy on his way home from church. He said the crowds around the gates were obscene, everyone screaming and begging the Americans to rescue them.

They're scared.

Ba Minh took the pan from Hoa's hand to slide the over-cooked egg onto a plate. They're panicking, she said. They've already turned on our government. Ba Minh's husband was a general in the South Vietnamese army. He'd mentored Hoa's husband when Lum first joined the army, which initiated the friendship between the two families. Ba Minh's patriotism was as fierce as any soldier's.

Hoa stood there as Ba Minh cracked more eggs into the pan. She realized she was in the way. Hoa stepped back, reaching for the baguettes on the tray, and began tearing them open.

What are your employers going to do?

The plan is still to evacuate the orphans.

There might not be time. Ba Minh opened a baguette and eased a cooked egg between the torn folds.

They want to try.

I don't understand how you can help this happen.

If Ba Minh was determined to fight about this, there was nothing Hoa could do but speak as respectfully and firmly as possible. She could understand the widow's argument, and if circumstances were different, Hoa would agree.

These children will be in danger if they stay, Hoa said.

But taking them out of their home country isn't dangerous? Ba Minh asked.

No one can care for them here.

And the Americans will?

Yes.

How do you know? What if they're not accepted? Those Americans hate us now. They thought we were a waste of time. Sending those innocent children to that country will be fatal.

The center has lists of American families willing to adopt. They want these children.

They don't know what they are getting. Maybe they think it's fashionable to purchase a souvenir of the war, but after the excitement is over, they will tire of the child, and what then? No one wants to raise a baby who isn't their own, especially if it's not even their own race.

Hoa concentrated on arranging the food on the plates. The eggs were cooling off already. That's not true.

We can care for our own, Ba Minh said, a stubborn frown tightening her face. There are plenty of good Vietnamese people who can adopt these children.

Hoa shook her head slowly. I see people leaving babies at the orphanage doorstep every day. No one wants to take a child in now, especially when we're losing a war.

Ba Minh looked stricken, and Hoa instantly regretted her words. She should have known better. Childless and widowed, Ba Minh now concentrated all that was left of her faith in the government. It made her feel proud and necessary when officials called for citizens to pray for their country. To lose the war was to destroy the last vestige of Ba Minh's family.

I smell bread!

They turned to see Cung and Van scamper into the courtyard. They ran up to the stove, happily salivating at the steaming food. Avoiding Hoa's gaze, Ba Minh instructed the boys to help take the prepared plates to the dining room. Hoa stayed behind, dragging a cloth along the stove with shaky hands.

Hoa wished she could take the widow to the orphanages, show her all the malnourished children, and ask her again if she still believed they wouldn't be better off in America. It was so easy for people like Ba Minh, who never had or wished for children, to decree where they should be raised and who should do it. They didn't know how many unwanted orphans there were in Vietnam. They had no idea.

Either they were stupid, or she was. The bureaucrats at the ministries couldn't decide who was in charge and saw nothing cruel in spinning Hoa from one office to the other. The Interior and Social Welfare ministries kept insisting that the other was in charge of approving and issuing passports and exit visas. Hoa had been through this runaround plenty before, but those were less urgent times. In the last week, the government had surrendered Hue, the cultural center of Vietnam. City officials couldn't contain reports of the thousands of Vietnamese dying as they tried to flee the enemy by boat, car, and foot. Those who could afford to legally leave on a plane were trying to do so. Hoa struggled to hold her own in these crowds, her arms heavy with folders stuffed with birth certificates and medical charts.

This morning should have been easier. They'd sent Steven along with her, hoping his imposing size would keep Hoa from getting bullied to the back of the crowds again. The center was also fearful of sending anyone downtown alone. Despite government pleas for citizens to remain calm, panic was spreading. Most of the open-air markets and street vendors had closed shop. People from the countryside were crowding the streets, exposing their wounds and absent limbs. Some clung to photographs of missing family members, frantically calling out their names.

With Steven beside her, Hoa tricked herself into remaining

calm. Only a few weeks into his arrival, Steven was already more comfortable at his job, his once naive eyes now saddled with a grim wariness. But while Steven's presence kept other petitioners from pushing Hoa around, it didn't impress the bureaucrats much.

Three months, the city official informed them after Hoa presented her cases.

We can't wait three months, Hoa said.

It takes a minimum of three months to review and process visa applications. The official wasn't even looking at them, her eyes darting between the two piles of applications weighing down the sides of her desk.

But I understand a rush can be ordered if there are doctors' statements on medical conditions—

The minister has ordered a halt on all rushes for the time being. If you'd like, you can speak to the Ministry of the Interior—

We were just there, Hoa said, her eyes gesturing to Steven, who sat next to her, ably performing his duty of looking impatient. I'd really like to handle this with Social Welfare.

There was a hard rap on the door. An older man poked his head in and glowered into the room.

Excuse me, the official said, standing up from her chair and leaving the room.

Hoa slumped back in the hard metal chair. The small office was poorly ventilated, with tiny desk fans that did little except flutter the papers occasionally. Through the office window, Hoa could see soldiers setting up sandbags and barbed wire along the Ministry building. They looked exhausted, foreheads shiny and uniforms stained with perspiration.

An army messenger had come by the house early one morning the previous week, bringing the news that half of Lum and

Tan's regiment was missing in action. He was careful to point out this did not mean they were dead. But if the army was so confident Lum and Tan were alive, they wouldn't need to send this boy to speak to her. Ba Minh, though, was convinced they had survived and urged Hoa to pray for the same, at least for the sake of her boys. But there wasn't time to think about what she did or didn't believe. The possibility that Lum and Tan were gone, that Hoa would have to raise her two sons alone as the Communists marched closer, was paralyzing. That couldn't happen. She had too much to do. In the last few weeks at the center, guards had sealed off the compound from despondent parents pleading to drop off their children. Hoa couldn't enter or leave the center without someone screaming at her to help their babies. Accusations of her cruel indifference hovered in her thoughts constantly.

Is she coming back? Steven asked after fifteen minutes had passed.

I don't know, Hoa said. But now that they'd finally made it into the office, she was not going to leave. She straightened her folders on the desk, a futile attempt to make them look more official. Most of the birth certificates and medical charts she'd brought had been forged at the center, a necessary guiltless crime, since most of their orphans had arrived without names or documentation. It was all part of the game. So these children could survive, Hoa somehow had to convince the government that they legally existed, were in legitimate danger, and needed to exit the country immediately.

This was the frustrating and crucial element of Hoa's job. She wasn't as good at tangling with bureaucrats as Sophie and other staff members. Her only advantage was trying to establish a bond through speaking Vietnamese, which rarely worked. Often, they were more suspicious of Hoa than the

Americans, not above implying that her appeal to send these children abroad was somewhat traitorous.

A few minutes later, the official strode in noticeably more confident, her back straight, eyes steady on Hoa's. She picked up the files Hoa had left on the table.

I will personally take these cases to the superior and express their urgency. Do you have legal copies of these documents?

Yes, Hoa said, looking askance at Steven, who appeared equally stunned. Of course.

I have a meeting with him in an hour. She held the files on her hip and smiled at Hoa and Steven. I will call you this afternoon, hopefully with good news.

Hoa and Steven hurried back to the orphanage, eager to surprise everyone with their inexplicable breakthrough at the ministries. When they pulled into the driveway, they saw the center's three other vans parked in front, their back doors open, jammed with boxes. Staff members were running to and from the vans with supplies and bottles in their arms.

President Ford made an agreement with the South Vietnamese government, Bridget yelled to them as they walked to the house. We get to leave today!

Hoa and Steven stared at each other. What happened? Hoa said.

Ask Sophie, Bridget said, pushing a box into the van with both hands. She talked to the Ministry this morning.

The adults' frantic activity had spread to the children, who ran around the house wildly, screaming about airplane rides and searching for lost toys and stuffed animals they wanted to take with them. In the kitchen, the cooks feverishly prepared formula bottles, while Thanh and a few others sat at the dining room table scribbling out identification bracelets for the children. Hoa and Steven made their way to Sophie's office. The floor was covered with files. Behind the desk, Sophie sat talking on a phone wedged between her ear and shoulder, while trying to sort a pile of papers on her lap.

We're only a half hour's drive away, Sophie said. No, I'm sure guards won't be necessary. . . . At the airport at four, got it . . . Thank you again, so much.

Her face split into a grin when she hung up the phone. You heard. It's a miracle, isn't it? She stood and began pacing the room, too excited to stay still. A military aircraft is waiting for us at the airport, she said. It's huge. We're sharing it with another agency.

So we have room for everyone?

Everyone who has paperwork.

That's great, Steven said. That must be why the bureaucrat promised us those passports and visas so quickly.

They're calling it the Operation Babylift, Sophie said. President Ford is promising they'll evacuate as many orphans as they can.

Looking back and forth between Sophie's and Steven's faces, Hoa hated to end their joy so soon, but there was no time to wait. Is the staff leaving, too? Hoa asked.

Sophie reached over to clasp Hoa's arm. Hon, the city is collapsing. It would be very dangerous for any American to stay.

Hoa nodded. She could feel their eyes on her, waiting for a more emotional reaction, maybe tears or wailing. But that wasn't her. They should have known that.

This doesn't mean we're going to leave friends behind, dear. Sophie moved closer to Hoa, her hand never leaving Hoa's arm. We want you to come with us.

Hoa looked up. Sophie's face was serious.

We're worried about your safety, too, Sophie said. You and all our Vietnamese staff. We plan to burn all the records before we leave, but that doesn't guarantee you won't be branded as traitors.

That's very generous of you, Hoa said, but I don't have any paperwork. You're going to have enough trouble evacuating the older children.

There are ways to exit you legally. Sophie took a breath. The easiest is by having you marry a U.S. citizen. She looked pointedly at Steven, who smiled softly at Hoa.

You've been such a help to me, Steven said. I'd love to help you if I can.

The whole staff is marrying each other, Sophie said. It's bizarre, but sweet, I think. I'm marrying Dang.

I can't, Hoa said. I'm already married.

Hon, Sophie said, reaching over to hold her other hand. Of course it wouldn't be a real marriage. It's just a trick, so we can get everyone to the States. This way, you can also bring your sons.

Hoa gently removed herself from Sophie's hands. But I'm already married.

Sophie and Steven exchanged glances. I would never tell you to give up on your husband, Sophie said. But you haven't heard anything for months now. You need to think about your safety and your boys.

It would just be a quick ceremony at the airport, Steven said. Father Do will perform a mass ceremony, and we sign a paper. It'll be barely legal enough to get us to the States.

He looked so eager to please, this young boy. Imagining the couple they'd make in front of the priest, a chubby, middle-aged Vietnamese woman and a skinny, red-haired American boy, Hoa could almost laugh.

This is, of course, entirely your decision, hon, Sophie said. I'm sorry you don't have much time to think about it. I just couldn't, in my heart, abandon you here without the choice.

Everyone on the American staff thought she should go and told her so. But Hoa needed to talk to someone who still saw Vietnam as home, a place not so easily forgotten.

I have to do this for my family, Thanh said, when Hoa took her aside in the hallway. Once I'm in America, I can petition to bring them out, too. Come with us, Hoa. Her eyes were pleading. Lum would want you to protect his sons.

Thanh looked away to stare into the dining room. Hoa followed her gaze to the toddlers standing in line, waiting for Bridget to examine them. Freshly bathed with neatly combed hair, they nudged and tickled each other, unaware of what would happen in several hours. They were so fortunate. These children would have the opportunity to live freely in America. What kind of mother would Hoa be if she had that chance for her sons and refused it?

Hoa borrowed Sophie's car to return home and gather her sons and essential belongings. It might have been easier to walk. The streets were cluttered with barricades and barbed wire, slowing Hoa to the pace of most pedestrians. Soldiers desperately tried to keep traffic under control, but the cars ignored their frenzied whistles and arm gestures. A few times, pedestrians slammed into the side of the car, forcing Hoa to stop, afraid she'd struck someone. But by the time Hoa rolled down the window, the crowd had already surged forward.

Over the city loudspeakers, officials reiterated the strict enforcement of an early curfew. Hoa drove by shattered storefront windows, where people fought over stolen radios and sewing machines. Burning trash cans lit random street corners. Above the city noise, she could still hear gunfire and ground explosions in the distance.

When she entered the house, she called out her sons' names, but no one answered. The bedroom was empty. She went out to the courtyard and called their names again. Then she heard it, sobbing, coming from Ba Minh's bedroom. Hoa ran to her door and opened it. Ba Minh sat on her bed, Hoa's sons on each side of her. They were all crying.

What happened? Hoa asked, slowly walking into the room.

Ba Minh's arms around the boys tightened. They're alive, she said.

Hoa looked at her older son. Van, she said.

It's true, Van said, holding up a letter. Daddy and Tan are alive.

Hoa took the wrinkled letter from his hands. It was her husband's scrawl. Only four lines long. He and Tan were in a prison camp in Hanoi. Tan had been sick with malaria and was slowly recovering. He didn't know how long they would be there, but they were alive. His only thoughts were of their family and returning to them.

Praise God, Ba Minh said. Hoa wasn't sure if she was laughing or crying. The widow hugged the children closer, and they squealed with delight. Praise God.

What's wrong, Mother? Cung asked, tugging on her pant leg.

I'm just happy, Hoa said, wiping her face with the back of her hand.

No, I mean, why are you home so early? Was work canceled?

No, son, Hoa said. Ba Minh looked up, and they smiled at each other. I missed my family, that's all.

Can we write a letter back? Do you think they will get it?

We can try.

Can we do it now?

No, not now. After I come home from work.

Behind the gates, the guards performed their final duties, keeping the crowds from spilling into the driveway. Hoa stood at the top of the villa's front steps. She waved with both hands as the vans and buses pulled away, smiling at the children pressing their palms against the back windows. When the cars turned off the street, the crowds around the gates slowly began to disperse.

Hoa and two other staff members who also decided to stay behind returned to the villa to finish cleaning up. They worked steadily into the evening. They packed leftover toys and supplies into boxes. They filled up trash bags and set them in piles in the atrium. They emptied the filing cabinets and burned the remaining files in the courtyard.

It was near dark when Hoa stepped out to the driveway. The area was near-quiet, people already hurrying home for the early curfew. Hoa walked around, picking up leftover trash and forgotten toys.

Are you sure? Thanh had asked, before stepping onto the bus. We could send someone to bring your boys to the airport.

I have to wait for Lum and Tan, Hoa said.

They're in prison. You don't know when or if they'll be released.

I won't leave them.

Stubborn Hoa, Thanh said, hugging her. I'm so scared for you.

There will be other planes, Hoa told herself. Other opportunities.

The guards locked the gates. The siren blew, and Hoa went inside.

EMANCIPATION

I NEVER KNEW MY *father and I barely remember my mother. When I was five years old, I was smuggled on a boat with forty-eight other refugees to escape Vietnam. We spent three weeks on the open sea, nearly starving, until a Norwegian naval ship rescued our leaky, water-rotted boat. I arrived in America with no family, no money, and no home. At the refugee center, I was labeled an unaccompanied minor and put in a foster home. I have been in one since then.*

Against sound advice, Mai did not look up. During her twenty minutes at the podium, she spoke clearly, articulately, and kept her head down, her eyes smoothing over the memorized words. Maintaining a comfortable balance between conversation and formal speech, Mai was confident she held most of the audience's attention. People bored by her lack of eye contact and charisma—lower classmen, jocks, snobs—were negligible. Those who were supposed to listen—teachers, faculty, friends—would do so whether or not she raised her head. They were enough.

The immediate environment tightened around her. The

static on the microphone. The occasional cough and shifting in the metal foldout chairs. Her shoes rubbing against the sweaty gymnasium floor. Losing her breath and needing to swallow at the end of every other sentence. If she looked up, she would see the audience's faces, realize what they thought, and be unable to finish.

Mai didn't like people looking at her. She excelled in academics, not appearance. When people stared, she assumed she didn't measure up, and Mai hated feeling inadequate, especially for things that were out of her control. She'd given up long ago trying to appear pretty. She reinvested her time and effort for more realistic ambitions.

The award for the school's best college essay was a five-hundred-dollar scholarship and a reading at the senior awards assembly. Mai didn't know about the latter until after she won. Admissions committees reading her personal statement was one thing, exposing it to her senior class was another.

You shouldn't apologize for having a hard life, her AP English teacher Mrs. Ward said, when Mai hesitated about reading. You've overcome a lot at such a young age, and you should be proud of that.

Back in September, Mrs. Ward encouraged the students to choose unique subjects for their personal statement, stories that would distinguish them from the pool of other applicants. Colleges liked essays on triumphing over adversity and learning important values from a life lesson. This was one section of the application that wasn't ruled by numbers or letter grades. They should take advantage of it. Many students had problems coming up with something to write. Mai didn't.

But Mai was dissatisfied with her first version. It initially sounded good on paper: orphaned refugee at five years old, living in foster homes all her life. But the truth was after moving in with Karen and Sherman Reynolds when she was nine, she was allowed a childhood, unlike her former foster brothers and sisters. Ultimately good, but not when you're trying to get into an Ivy League school. Her situation turned out so fortunate that she had nothing to write about. It was strange, realizing her life had to be worse to count for something.

So she played it up. Remembering all the sympathies people had projected on her all her life, Mai wrote of her longing for her dead mother and native land and her resolution to return to Vietnam one day and help her former countrymen. Though difficult at first to exaggerate her emotions in such a way, Mai was soon swept up in the embellishments. Perhaps she really did think this, Mai considered as she admired the finished printout. Mrs. Ward was thrilled after reading it, almost crying, pushing away any doubts Mai had about its integrity.

The applause and sympathetic smiles afterward indicated the audience thought so, too. Mai nodded tightly as Principal Baldwin patted her shoulder. When he had introduced her at the assembly, he proudly listed all the schools she'd already been accepted to, the scholarships they offered, declaring her such a lucky girl with fortunate opportunities. He probably meant to be complimentary, but the words bristled her ego. Lucky. Fortunate. Had he talked to the school counselor? Did he know that Mai was still waiting on Wellesley? Did he think she was being ungrateful? It wasn't luck. Yes, she was once the poor orphan child, but she had earned this. Since middle school, she had worked to ensure a future other children already inherited.

The Reynoldses were easy to find, Sherman, with his long red ponytail, and Karen's frizzy gray hair. The third row in the right section, they waved her over. Mai tried to discourage them from coming. They'd have to take time off from work since it was during the middle of the day. She also wasn't sure how they'd react to the essay. But they insisted, especially since it was such a special occasion. When Mai reached the Reynoldses, Karen immediately splayed her arms out, one hand dangling a tissue.

I had no idea, Karen whispered in Mai's ear as they hugged. That was beautiful.

It's just an essay, Mai said. They were staring at her, amazed at what twenty minutes had revealed that nine years previously hadn't.

We are so proud of you, Sherman said.

Students streamed out of the auditorium, slowly, reluctantly returning to classes. Mai sat in an empty folding chair. Has the mail come? she asked.

Karen shook her head. You know we'd tell you if something arrived.

Of course Mai's top choice was the last school to get back to her. She was currently wait-listed at Wellesley. They said they'd have a decision on admission and financial aid in several weeks. That was two months ago. Since then, Mai had reviewed the application in her head over and over, searching for the flaw that was keeping her admission in this miserable limbo. Although not wealthy, the Reynoldses lived in a good school district, with one of the most competitive high schools in the county. Mai's transcript was impeccable: honors and AP classes, A's and A minuses, with only a few B pluses from the sciences, but she was applying as a humanities major. Her extracurricular activities (student government, yearbook, track and field) were decorated with commendations and awards. Despite being unable to afford expensive SAT prep courses, she scored well above the Wellesley average. The teachers who wrote her letters of recommendation adored her. The only part left was the personal statement.

Let's not think about that today, Sherman said, reaching over to squeeze Mai's arm warmly. All right? It's your birthday. We should celebrate.

It's not that important, Mai said.

Nonsense, he said. Eighteen is a landmark year. Adulthood. You'll never forget it.

When will dinner with your friends be over? Karen asked.

You guys don't have to do anything for me, Mai said.

We know we don't have to, Sherman said, with a grin. But I've already made the cake. It would be rude for you not to indulge us one more time.

It was a Reynolds tradition. There was a homemade cake for every birthday in the house since Mai moved in with them. Mai remembered first meeting the Reynoldses, her shock that they were white and vegetarian. She initially thought the social worker had placed her there because she was mad at her. Mai didn't know what a genuine, safe home felt like.

I'll be home at ten, Mai said. Eleven at the latest.

I can't believe you'll be going off to college soon, Karen marveled.

From across the gymnasium, Mai's friend Tiffany smiled and waved. Tiffany had already been accepted to Wellesley. They were planning to room together.

Me neither, Mai said.

She said good-bye to the Reynoldses in the parking lot. They agreed she'd be home by ten o'clock for cake and presents. Her gaze skimmed over the student parking section, full of SUVs and imports, likely their parents' hand-me-down cars or birthday gifts.

Mai never liked birthdays. She hated attention, the scrutiny and judgment, and that was what birthdays were for. There was an expectation to have fun that she resented. For Mai, to make the day special and glorious was too much pressure, the probability of failure so imminent. Then a person was left with only disappointment. Mai had more important things to think about. She couldn't worry about making one day worthwhile.

Across the street from campus, Kim waved to her, casually leaning against a car that wasn't hers. Mai looked around, hoping the car's owner wasn't close by.

Kim still wore her work uniform, her long brown ponytail poking from the rear opening of the baseball cap. Though sweaty and tired, Kim still looked beautiful. Mai caught her own inadequate reflection in the car window and looked away.

You got off early, Mai said.

It wasn't too hard. Kim stared at her. I'm coming in earlier on Saturday. What's wrong?

Nothing.

You sure?

Mai nodded. I was going to come by the restaurant.

I figured. Are you going somewhere?

No.

Want to sit out?

Sure.

They walked in silence to a park several blocks from the school. They sprawled out in the grass, stretching their legs in front of them.

What is it, Mai? Kim said. Just say it.

So Mai tried, but the same thing happened that always did whenever she tried to talk to Kim about her college plans. Kim's eyes wandered, her responses became curt, her obvious disinterest and disdain unapologetically obvious. There was no point. Mai bent forward to fix the laces on her tennis shoes, when Kim leaned over to brush some hair from Mai's eyes.

You used to be so little, Kim said. Not anymore.

I think I'm still growing. Maybe I'll grow taller than you.

I don't think so.

Kim was Mai's oldest friend. They had lived in several foster homes together, sharing a bed when there weren't enough. Two years older, Kim was an older sister to Mai, shielding her from the viciousness of foster siblings and foster parents.

Though Mai eventually found a home with the Reynoldses, Kim never found hers. She never stayed in one place longer than two years. It wasn't supposed to be that way. Kim was meant to be luckier. She came over to the States as part of the Babylift evacuation and was promptly adopted by an American family. But the family had given her back, something about not realizing how difficult it would be to raise a foreign child. Social Services put Kim in a foster home, which is where Mai met her.

Even more than Karen and Sherman, Mai was going to miss Kim when she left for college. Her foster parents would be fine without her, but she wasn't sure about Kim. She'd taken their first separation hard. One of the few times Mai had seen Kim cry was when the social worker, Mrs. Luong, split them up: Kim, Mai, and Vinh, this boy who'd been with them since the beginning. Mai didn't mind separating from Vinh. But she did regret leaving Kim behind.

So did the Reynoldses get you anything?

I don't know.

They will, Kim said. They always have. She looked around the park, her attention drifting to two boys pushing each other on a swing set. Think they're going to miss you?

Miss me?

Yeah.

I guess. Maybe.

I think they will, Kim said.

Well, they're getting another foster kid after I leave.

Really?

Yeah. Mai tugged at a handful of grass. It's not a big deal. They had another kid living there before me, too.

Yeah, but you guys were so close, Kim said. What's that? With her foot, she nudged Mai's misshapen backpack, where the award lay wedged inside.

Nothing, Mai said.

Did you get another prize? Kim sang. C'mon, they're hilarious. Show me.

Mai reluctantly pulled out the award. Kim held it with both hands, smudging her fingerprints over the gold-plated plaque. You never showed me your essay.

Really? Mai took the award from her and shoved it into her backpack. I thought I did.

No. Bring a copy to dinner tonight.

Mai sat up a little. We're having dinner?

Aren't we?

But . . . we never talked about it.

Kim turned on her side, facing Mai. I thought it was assumed.

I . . . I didn't know. I sort of already made plans.

Seriously? Kim narrowed her eyes. With who?

Huan and Tiffany. Huan is home for spring break, and they're taking me to dinner.

Oh. Kim returned to lying on her back, staring at cloudless sky.

Kim, Mai said.

She looked at Mai, her chin pointed high, her eyes hard.

Mai hated when she did that. Kim had this way of looking at her, making Mai feel either wanted or unnecessary, depending on whim. Mai couldn't even invite Kim along. Kim thought Tiffany giggled too much. And she couldn't stand Huan. Mai had introduced them to each other a few years ago, thinking they'd get along because they were both Babylift orphans. Maybe they'd been on the same plane. But Mai had forgotten a crucial difference. Huan's adoptive parents kept him. Kim would speak in Vietnamese whenever Huan was around, always claiming to forget that he only understood English.

Come on, Mai said, trying to poke Kim in the ribs.

What? Kim said, harshly brushing her hand away. You have plans with your other friends. Okay.

Dinner isn't going to take long. Do you want to do something after?

You don't have to.

I want to.

Are you sure?

Yes.

I know you, Mai. Don't lie to me. No one will ever know you like I do.

I know.

Mrs. Luong had warned Mai that the Reynoldses were white.

This is good, she said. Their last foster child was Chinese, and he did well with them. You can practice your English and do better in school.

Already shy, Mai hid behind Mrs. Luong's legs. The green front door opened and their smiling faces peered out, presenting confusion: the man's hair was long, and the woman's hair was short. They looked too young and thin to be foster parents. Mai clutched the social worker's hand instinctively.

Too strange for handshakes and too soon for hugs, they simply smiled and nodded at each other as Mrs. Luong introduced everyone. The Reynoldses stared unabashedly as Mai fidgeted, examined her new surroundings, pulled on her hair, straightened her shirt. Their scrutiny made Mai reconsider her frustrations of being ignored at other foster homes.

Their furniture looked clean and comfortable. She noticed immediately there was no television in the living room. They showed Mai her room, her own private room, with a twin bed and dresser and nightstand and bookshelves. There was already a small set of books stacked neatly on the top shelf. She looked through all of them. They were for her reading age level.

When Mai returned to the living room, she could tell Mrs. Luong had been talking about her. The young couple's smiles were gone, and their gazes, once merely genial, seemed more intense and weighted. Self-conscious, Mai put her hands behind her back, hoping they wouldn't ask to look at her wrists like the social worker did.

Show them you're a good girl, Mrs. Luong had whispered to her before leaving.

There were doubts, of course. She'd never been in a foster home by herself before, let alone with a non-Vietnamese family who ate food unfamiliar to Mai. But there was a sense of security in this home she'd never experienced before, and she realized this was what it was supposed to be like. The past had been the deviant, the wrong, but it was over.

Tiffany's parents co-owned a seafood restaurant in Newport Beach that offered a panoramic view of the ocean and Orange County. Mai and her friends sat at a table by the window and toasted champagne glasses full of ginger ale. They split orders of lobster, mahimahi, and shrimp, so they could sample all the dishes. Mai brushed away invisible bread crumbs from the front of her dress, carefully gathering them in her palm to deposit in her napkin.

This time next year we won't be playing grown-up, Tiffany said.

C'mon, Huan said. I'm still living off my parents, and so will you.

But not with them, Tiffany said. We'll be on the other side of the country.

Huan looked at Mai. Have you heard from Wellesley?

Mai shook her head.

There's still a lot of time, Tiffany said. My brother didn't hear from Brown until almost June.

They both smiled at her, their futures secure with Huan attending Brown and Tiffany's acceptance to Wellesley. Huan and Tiffany had attended the same private elementary school before meeting Mai in high school. Mai met Huan first while taking Latin, the only Vietnamese students in their class. Huan and Tiffany didn't even bother filling out FAFSA forms or applying for scholarships. It was so easy for them. They had no idea how much more work it was doing everything by yourself.

When they first began looking at colleges, Huan and Tiffany had convinced Mai to consider the East Coast, not only for the education, but for the opportunity of living elsewhere. Growing up wasn't only about classes, but life experience, and they'd already lived in California. Since her escape from Vietnam, Mai had never left the state. When she told the Reynoldses of her college ambitions, Karen encouraged her to apply to Wellesley. She showed Mai her old college yearbooks, reminiscing about the close attention she received since it was such a small school. Gazing at the slightly faded photographs of smiling young women, Mai easily imagined a home there.

We'll finally get to experience seasons, Tiffany said, reaching over for Mai's plate to fork another shrimp. We should take a road trip to see the leaves change color.

I'll have a car by then, Huan said. I can pick you and Mai up, and we'll drive along the coast.

Her teachers, though, advised her to apply to some safety schools in the state, which Mai did. But she was confident in the private institutions she applied to and the minority scholarships available to finance them. She stacked the college brochures neatly on her desk beside her textbooks, looking at them occasionally as further motivation to continue studying.

When the results came in, Mai knew she should have been more grateful, but she couldn't fight off the disappointment. While she gained admission into top choices like Sarah Lawrence and Cornell, the financial aid packages they offered weren't nearly enough to cover projected costs. Wellesley was her last chance.

My fraternity sponsors a ski trip to Vermont every year, Huan said. They rent out a block of condos for the long weekend. You guys should come.

You've never been in snow, have you? Tiffany said, turning to Mai.

Mai didn't answer, engrossed in squeezing the lemon slice from her water glass. The restaurant was lit with tea candles and torch lights, imbuing the tables with a gauzy orange glow. This was a setting for romantic dinners, not high school birthdays.

When Mai looked up, she caught Huan and Tiffany exchanging glances, perhaps finally noticing how little she'd spoken throughout dinner.

Mai, what is it? Huan asked.

I can't talk about it anymore. I know you guys are excited, but I don't know what's going to happen next year. So I can't really make plans for road trips and ski weekends.

Don't worry, Tiffany said. You'll hear from Wellesley soon.

I might not. And even if I do, I have no idea how I'm going to pay for it.

You'll get a scholarship. And the Reynoldses will help you.

No they won't.

Of course they will.

No. Really. I'm eighteen. I'm officially emancipated. They're no longer obligated by the state to support or even shelter me after today.

Mai had never told them about this before. They knew very little about the foster care system, and she'd always preferred it that way. Tiffany and Huan kept looking at each other. Mai wanted to yell that she could see them, the patronizing eyes they shared.

They're not going to kick you out, are they? Huan asked.

No. But I don't know if I'm coming to their house for my school breaks. There might not be room after they get another foster child. They have no responsibility to me.

It's not about responsibility, Tiffany said. They love you. They'll want you to visit.

Mai looked out the window at the blinking lights of the city. The dark slopes of the hills where the wealthy of Orange County hovered. There would be cake soon, but Mai was too full, she didn't want any. And she especially didn't want to be sung to.

Mrs. Luong had told Mai long ago that the Reynoldses were interested in foster care, not adoption. They wanted to help as many children as they could. Mai understood this, most of the time. But there were other times she thought she could change their minds. She did everything to demonstrate she'd make a nice daughter. She listened to them, never disobeyed house rules, and always respected curfew. The Reynoldses talked about how proud they were of Mai, what a fine person she was. That was where their admiration ended. They had so many years to make her a legitimate part of their family, but the possibility was never even discussed.

And if Wellesley accepted me, they have to take you, Tiffany said.

Why? Mai asked, finally returning her gaze to her friends.

Are you kidding? Huan said. Your grades are even better than mine were. And I read your essay.

Mai remembered Huan's college essay. She still had a copy of it somewhere, used it as inspiration to write hers. He talked about being an orphan. She was shocked when she first read it, since Huan never talked about his feelings about being adopted. His essay's authority stemmed from his sincerity. Hers didn't have that.

It is an advantage that you're an orphan, Tiffany whispered, leaning forward like it was a terrible secret. Even though I know it must have been really, really hard. There's no way they can reject you after what you told them about your childhood.

You need to have faith in yourself, Huan said. And relax.

For dessert, their server set a slice of tiramisu cake with one candle in front of Mai. She gazed at the small, flickering flame as her friends and the waiter sang "Happy Birthday." They told her to make a wish. She blew out the candle.

This is good, Mai said when the car slowly approached the curb.

Huan looked at the dark apartment building skeptically. Are you sure? You don't want me to wait until you get in?

No, see right there? Mai pointed to the lit window above. I can tell she's home. She looked at Huan. Want to come with me?

I don't think so, he said. Thanks anyway.

Besides Mai, Huan had no other Vietnamese friends. Mai wondered if they'd even be friends if she hadn't introduced herself during their first class together. Huan got so nervous around other Vietnamese—convinced since he was only half and raised by white parents, he wouldn't know how to talk to them.

Mai hesitated as she reached for the door handle of Huan's jeep. I lied. In the essay.

Huan stared at her for a moment. I don't think so. I know you. I read that essay, and I believe you.

Everyone believed me, but it isn't true. Do you miss your biological mother?

Huan looked out his window. They never talked about it, their shared history as orphans. They were always too busy with plans for the future, their new lives. When he didn't say anything, Mai believed she had her answer.

Well, neither do I. I made it all up. I'm an opportunist. It's pathetic.

I do miss her, Huan said. It's a small part of me, but it's there. I think that part of you wrote the essay.

Mai shook her head. I never think about her.

But you had to, Huan said. You couldn't avoid it. You were writing about her.

Mai didn't respond. It seemed too easy. He was offering her an excuse for her behavior, an honorable and justified explanation. She didn't deserve it.

Give me a call if you can't get a ride home, Huan said, when she opened her door. Even if it's late.

Mai ran up the pathway to the front of the building, pressing the buzzer for the correct apartment. When the gate gave, she entered the building. She heard Huan's car finally drive away.

Mai walked through the neglected courtyard, full of brown bushes and rusty, peeling benches. It was a two-story complex with thin walls, so it could get noisy. This wasn't even Kim's apartment. The lease was with her old foster sister Luan. Kim had moved in a month ago, after leaving Vinh. She was trying to convince Luan to let her stay since Kim couldn't afford her own place.

Mai would stay for a half hour, long enough to be polite. Nothing more. The Reynoldses were expecting her home soon. She didn't want to tell them where she was because they would want to pick her up, and Mai didn't want them to see where Kim lived.

She could hear the music from down the hall. Mai pushed on the door, already slightly open. The living room was full of people. No one turned when she slipped in.

Hey, Kim said, emerging from the crowd. She wore a glittery dark blue halter, slim black pants, and an unusually big smile on her face. It's about time.

I didn't know it was a party. Mai tugged at her lavender dress self-consciously. What seemed appropriate for dinner felt silly and childish now.

It's a big day, Kim said. You're an adult now, you're free.

Oh. Mai didn't recognize half the people in the room.

We're all here to celebrate with you, Kim said, throwing her arms around Mai.

Mai scrutinized her friend as they separated. Kim was never affectionate unless she'd been drinking.

Are you going to be able to drive me home tonight?

Sure. Luan said I could use her car.

But can you?

God, don't lecture me. I just need a couple hours.

They walked into the kitchen where Luan was making drinks. The linoleum floor stuck to Mai's heels from spilled beer.

Here she is, Luan said, looking up briefly to smile at them. What do you want to drink?

Mai shook her head.

Come on, Kim said, leaning over the kitchen counter, kicking her bare feet up behind her. It's your birthday.

Mai smiled politely. I'm fine.

What? Luan's face twisted, confused. She often did this, pretended she couldn't understand Mai's Vietnamese accent.

I said I'm fine, Mai said loudly in English.

That's cool, Luan said. It is a school night for you.

Mai nodded and ducked her head, looking back into the living room. Kim and Luan had lived in a foster home together during high school. While Luan was always nice to her, Mai had the feeling she only tolerated her because of Kim. No matter how many years Mai gained, she'd always feel like a little kid with the two of them, never able to catch up.

Did you bring your essay? Kim asked. When Mai didn't answer, she rolled her eyes. I didn't think so. You know, Mai, I do know how to read, if that's what you're worried about.

I'll give it to you later.

Oh, forget it. I don't care anymore.

Kim introduced her to some people, most of them old foster brothers and sisters. These were Kim's friends, but she presented them like Mai had also grown up with them. Over the loud music, they smiled politely, tipping their beer bottles, some shouting happy birthday. Every few minutes, Mai would look at her watch, then at Kim. It was getting late, but she didn't want to leave until Kim was sober.

The party grew thicker with people, the front door opening and closing to let in more, but no one out. Mai was taking in the room again while Kim talked with Luan, when she recognized a new guest.

Mai pulled on Kim's arm until she looked, too.

Did you invite him? Mai asked.

Nooo, Kim said, shaking her head vigorously.

Mai hadn't seen Vinh in several months. Since then, he'd shaved his head, making him look skinnier than ever. He stood alone, which was strange. He usually never went anywhere without Hung, his older foster brother, another gang punk. Vinh caught Mai looking at him, so she quickly glanced away.

Then why don't you ask him to leave?

I don't know, Kim said, now tipping her head to the beat of the music. He had some fallout with his boys. Really harsh. I don't want to make him feel worse.

Why do you care?

Come on. You don't have to talk to him.

Mai knew that. She just didn't want Kim to. For reasons Mai couldn't understand, Kim liked Vinh, even though he was a bully, a high school dropout, and, best of all, a gang member. Unfortunately, they had dated for years.

Mai tried steering them in Vinh-free areas of the party, but he seemed to inch closer, a patient, diligent stalker. Mai had put it off long enough and finally had to use the bathroom, choosing the one in Luan's room that had less traffic. When she returned to the party, sure enough, Vinh had cornered Kim at the kitchen door. She looked bored as he leaned close, whispering in her ear, but she wasn't moving away either.

Mai walked up to them and waited until Kim finally noticed her.

Can you take me home? Mai asked, looking only at her friend.

Hey, Vinh said, staring Mai up and down. Little girl finally grew up.

You want to leave? Kim asked. You just got here.

Not really, it's almost midnight.

But it's your birthday. No it's more than that, it's your emancipation day. Freedom from this damn state. No more visits or lectures from the social worker. Right, Vinh?

Yeah, he said. You can do whatever you want, whenever. No one hassling you.

That's right! Kim said. You could even move out! Do you want to? We could get a place together. It would be so fun, just like when we were kids.

When Luan walked by, Mai grabbed her arm. Can you take me home?

Luan shook her head. I can't drive.

Mai, I said I'd drive you home, Kim said. Just wait a minute.

I want to leave now, I have a headache.

A headache! Why?

I've got a lot on my mind.

God, are you still obsessing over that school in New York?

Massachusetts.

Oh whatever, it's still far away.

Why do you want to leave OC, Mai? Luan asked, looping her arm around Kim's waist. Their outfits almost matched. There are plenty of schools here.

She thinks she's too smart for them, Kim said.

Mai looked at Kim.

It's true, Kim said. It's what you think, I know it.

She's always been like that, huh? Vinh said.

She wants a life away from here. Kim smiled sweetly at Mai, her face angelic. Mai wants to get away from who she is.

There's nothing wrong with wanting to grow up, Mai said.

Honey, it's not that great, Kim said, leaning on Luan, barely able to stand anymore.

Mai took a breath, suddenly aware of everyone's eyes upon her, waiting for her to crumble. She focused her gaze on Kim. And how would you know?

They stared at each other, the others, everyone else at the party, briefly fading away. Then Kim pointed to the door. Get out. Get out right now.

Hey, Luan said.

You come into my house and talk to me like that? Kim said.

Whose house?

While Kim could appear cold to Mai, she'd never before looked hateful. It didn't feel real, the vicious words that slipped from their mouths so easily and quickly.

Out, Kim said. Her hazel eyes were rimmed in red. Or I will throw you out.

Shhh, Luan said, and turned to Mai, almost smugly. Maybe you should leave.

Without saying anything, Mai walked away. Every step required concerted effort to keep from falling. She found her purse buried underneath a pile of jackets in the living room. As she turned to leave, she saw Kim sitting on the couch, her hands covering her face. Luan and Vinh sat on each side of her.

At the pay phone outside, Mai called for a cab. She considered calling Huan, but realized she couldn't face anyone she knew. She sat on the curb, careful to avoid the rotten gummy areas, and waited. Mai realized she was shaking. They'd never fought like that before. She considered going back, apologizing, explaining herself, but she was suddenly afraid of facing all those people inside. She once belonged with them, but not anymore. Mai wouldn't know what to say.

When she heard footsteps on the gravel, she sat up.

Mai looked away when Vinh stood in front of her. I'm not getting in a car with you.

I wasn't offering. He shook his head at her, a thin smile on his face.

Mai stood up and backed a few steps, bumping into the bus stop sign. Go upstairs, she said.

Does it feel good making Kim cry like that?

I didn't mean to upset her.

No, you never mean to.

You know nothing about it.

I don't know why, but Kim always defended you. Even after you left us for those white hippies, she still said you were one of us.

I should have stayed and let you terrorize me?

That's right. You got your American dream family by selling us out. Telling everyone I was beating you.

You were.

Oh, come on. Really, Mai, how could that happen with Kim protecting you all the time?

It did. She glared at him. You found ways, I remember.

Okay. Maybe as kids we fought a little. But do you think a kid smacking you a few times even compares to what Kim's gone through?

It's not a contest.

But you won. Do you think it's fair what happened to Kim and never to you?

You can't blame me for that.

That's no one's fault, right? Just the luck of the draw who your foster parents are. Tell me, what makes you so pure and special?

Who's saying I am? She turned away from him, reminding herself that Vinh was a nobody, an uneducated high school dropout, an idiot gang member who preyed on the weak to feel strong. He thought she was weak, always had, but Mai had to show that she wasn't.

And are you still so clean? He skipped around, standing in front of her, invading her personal space, so she couldn't ignore him. Probably not or you'd be adopted by now. Don't you ever wonder why those hippies never adopted you? Why no one ever wanted to have you?

Mai wiped her eyes with the back of her hand. Vinh kept trying to look at her, so she hung her head low, allowing her hair to shield her eyes.

She would never tell him. How could she tell anyone? She has never been touched, kissed, even out of lust, violence, or pity.

Mai forced herself to lift her head, which felt heavy. Vinh was smirking, triumphant. You know nothing about my life, she said. You have no idea.

You're wrong. You may be smart, little girl. But don't think you're any better. Today, you've been released into the world, just like the rest of us.

I am better than you, Mai said. You're a nobody.

Vinh lunged forward, his hands clenching into fists. Mai twisted around, her arms covering her face.

Don't worry, Vinh said, waving his hands in the air, smiling. There must be a reason no one's touched you. I wouldn't dare.

The first time Kim spent the night at the Reynoldses', she gingerly touched everything in the house, as Mai had in the beginning. She was nervous around the Reynoldses, only speaking Vietnamese, even when they asked her questions, so that Mai had to translate.

You're staying, aren't you? Kim whispered, when they were under the covers, supposed to be asleep. For several weeks, Kim believed their separation was only temporary, and Mrs. Luong would find another home for them to be together again.

Mai pressed her face into the fresh pillowcase. I think so.

I guess it's not so bad here, Kim said. They seem okay for white people.

Yeah.

Maybe Mrs. Luong will find me a home like this.

Mai turned over so she faced her friend. You don't like it at the Buis?

I don't know. The woman's okay, she doesn't yell as much as Ba Kanh. But the man's weird.

Why?

He looks at me funny. He's always saying how pretty I am.

Mai didn't answer. Everyone was always telling Kim that. One time at the grocery store, this Vietnamese grandma called

Mai pretty, but Mai was sure the old lady said that to every child, even the ugly ones.

And he goes to the bathroom when I'm taking a shower.

Mai wrinkled her nose. Don't you lock the door?

Something's wrong with it. I tried putting the wastebasket against the door, but he knocked it over. Sometimes it's not just to pee, sometimes he craps in the toilet.

Eww!

I know.

Does he leave before you get out?

Kim hesitated. No.

Did you tell Mrs. Luong?

Uh-uh. I don't know, it's so gross.

Yeah.

They were silent. Mai returned to lying on her back. She could feel Kim's deep breaths next to her. She stared at the ceiling of this room, her room, where Karen and Sherman always knocked before entering. All those homes before, she'd escaped. But Kim had not, and Mai didn't know how to go back for her.

The house was dark. The Reynoldses were asleep. Mai dropped her purse on the kitchen counter and stood over the sink. Her headache dug into her temples, the blood roaring in her ears. She could feel the floor turning below her, gliding up the walls. Mai closed her eyes, waiting for the house to settle.

Mai traced her fingers over the clean counter surface. The previous summer, the Reynoldses had spent thousands of dollars renovating the kitchen. They expanded the pantry closet. They replaced the tiles and installed an island stove. They decided on a Provençal blue-and-yellow color scheme. Their next project was the living room.

Heavy footsteps on the stairs. Mai stared at the dark reflection of the kitchen window. Her eyes were swollen. The carefully ironed curls in her hair now appeared limp and flat.

Mai? What happened? Sherman asked, coming into the kitchen. Why are you home so late?

It went later than I expected, Mai said, rubbing her mouth with a dish towel.

We called Tiffany and Huan. They were home hours ago.

I went to see Kim. It was a surprise party.

Well why didn't you call us when you knew that?

The pain seeped into her eyes. Mai curled her fingers over the counter's edge, but couldn't prevent herself from sliding to the floor.

Sherman knelt beside her, a look of concern bruising his face. Are you sick? What did you drink?

Mai shook her head. I didn't drink anything.

It's okay if you did, Mai, it's your birthday, and you wanted to celebrate. Just tell me what—

I said I didn't drink. I'm not lying, okay?

Mai, you're yelling.

And what do you mean it's okay if I drink? What dad says that? You wouldn't say that if I was your real daughter.

Why are you so upset? What happened?

Nothing, okay? Nothing that wasn't supposed to, so don't worry about it. I'm not your responsibility anymore.

Come on. Let's get up. You need some water. He started to put his arms around her to help lift her up, but Mai screamed, slapping his hands away.

Don't touch me! Don't you ever touch me like that.

She sat on the floor, her arms crossed protectively over her chest, and watched, unblinking, as his face slowly began to change. Mai realized she should say something, anything, to keep his face from doing that. But she couldn't. He stood up, looking away, his shoulders stiff.

You should go to sleep. His voice was emotionless and unfamiliar. You have school tomorrow. He turned and walked out of the kitchen.

Mai waited and listened to his footsteps on the stairs and the careful opening and shutting of the master bedroom door. She imagined muffled conversation floating through the ceiling, Sherman shaking Karen awake and telling her what happened, her horror and disbelief, but eventual acceptance and disappointment.

Trying to breathe slowly, deeply, Mai pulled herself off the floor. With gentle steps, she made her way through the kitchen. As she pressed her palm against the light switch, she recognized the neatly arranged presents on the kitchen table. No doubt if she opened the refrigerator, there would be the homemade birthday cake wrapped in aluminum foil. Something on the table caught her eye. She leaned forward, her eyes focusing. A large white envelope posed next to the presents. Wellesley College. Mai pressed the light switch off. She went upstairs to bed.

Tell me about her, Kim said. She knew Mai hadn't fallen asleep yet. Tell me again. Exactly.

This was a nightly ritual when they used to live together. Kim was fascinated that Mai had known her mother. Mai would say what she could, trying hard to recall, but she'd been so young. If what Mai remembered wasn't enough to satisfy

Kim, she'd make up more details. It didn't matter if the attributes contradicted each other from one night to the next. Kim just wanted a picture in her head, shrouding her, before she went to sleep.

I believe she was beautiful. She looked like what I hope to look like when I grow up. Long, shiny black hair, small shoulders, golden skin, thin, elegant hands. She could have been more than what became of her. She should have lived longer, pursued a higher education than grade school level, seen her daughter grow up, lived in a country that didn't expect suffering, experienced a comfortable bed, clean food, and a day off. Because she never had any of these things, I will take them for her. I will live the way she should have.

BOUND

THEIR FINGERNAILS DUG INTO her shirtsleeves, creating fresh scrapes and irritating older ones. They grabbed for her hands, yanked at her hair, but Bridget didn't slow her stride. Her eyes remained focused on the black iron gate. She knew that once past it, she would be safe. The crowds around the orphanage would remain behind on the street. She'd walk up the driveway and through the building's front door without looking back.

She smoothly navigated through the tearful faces and pleading words, both Vietnamese and English. One woman tried to push a baby at her, but Bridget quickly deflected it, crossing her arms and shaking her head. It wasn't that she didn't sympathize, but there were enough children inside the center, the legitimate orphans they did accept, who needed her help.

As Bridget pushed open the gate, someone let out a scream above the crowd noise. She turned around. The woman was pressing the baby against the rusty bars of the gate.

Please, the woman cried in English.

Bridget shook her head. The baby squirmed, its face burning red against the yellowed newspaper it was wrapped in. Please, please.

Bridget forced herself to walk up the steps. When she reached the front door, an unusual silence drifted over the crowd. She looked back reluctantly, one hand grasping the doorknob.

People in the crowd stared toward a point in the concrete. The baby lay twisted on the center's side of the gate. The crowd started shouting again. The newspaper had fluttered off, leaving the child naked and exposing her gender. Her mouth was open, crying, but the crowd drowned her out.

Bridget immediately ran forward, carefully gathering the child into her arms, gingerly feeling for broken bones. The infant had scrapes on her limbs and deep scratches on her face. She needed to go to the hospital. There could be internal injuries.

She lifted the child from the ground and felt the crowd's eyes on her. Surrounding her.

Don't! Bridget yelled. She couldn't recall enough Vietnamese to say any more than that. So she kept repeating this as she slowly backed toward the center, her eyes searching their stunned faces. The mother had already disappeared.

Several staff members met her at the front door. They'd heard the commotion. Bridget yelled for them to move away so the infant could breathe. Someone left to bring the van around to the front of the house. One of the nurses checked the infant's breathing as Bridget held her. The child hardly weighed anything in Bridget's arms.

At the hospital, the doctors determined the infant had suffered a concussion, but in her weakened state of malnutrition and severe dehydration, survival through the night was uncertain. The hospital offered to observe the infant overnight, but Bridget knew that only meant a nurse would check on the child every hour or so. She needed closer surveillance.

Bridget returned with the infant and placed her in the orphanage's ICU upstairs. She assigned a nurse to watch the child, and Bridget checked on her periodically during daily rounds. After her shift, Bridget pulled a metal folding chair to the girl's crib and sat. She remembered Chelsea at this age, her rosy complexion and plump, soft skin.

One of the Vietnamese nurses, Chi, approached them late in the night to replenish the girl's IV. Sophie is hiring guards, she said. She is afraid this might encourage others.

That's good, Bridget said.

They are getting so desperate, Chi said, shaking her head.

Bridget concentrated on focal points that could eat time away: creaking ceiling fans, geckos crawling up the walls, the cracked veins along the once pristine tile floor, tiny bubbles floating up the IV bottle. She studied the girl's vitals with suspicion. She waited an hour, then another hour, until a member of the morning staff, Hoa, arrived with a formula bottle. The girl rolled on her side, mouth eagerly accepting the plastic nipple.

Realization seeped into Bridget's body thoroughly, soothing the tension that had gripped her muscles for hours. She felt Hoa's hands close over her shoulders, trying to absorb some of the shaking.

The baby is alive, Hoa said. This is good.

Bridget could only nod. She didn't know how to express it. This little girl's survival somehow felt better, more cathartic, than giving birth itself.

It was a television news special on the war, a feature story buried between battle segments. Vietnamese and Amerasian children in orphanages across Vietnam. The camera zoomed in on the orphans' faces and stayed there, allowing their sunken cheeks to fill the fourteen-inch television screen, casting thin shadows along the living room walls.

When his wife turned on the news special after dinner, she looked to Ronald to see if she should change the channel. Ronald had had a tour of duty in Vietnam, but he'd returned years ago, mind and body relatively intact. He nodded. This would be fine. Ten minutes later, he changed his mind.

Their little faces were gaunt, limbs so thin and frail, ballooned stomachs full only of air. While Ronald had seen this before firsthand, his wife hadn't. Bridget said nothing during the program, her gaze transfixed on the children. His wife was a pediatrician, and Ronald imagined her diagnosing each orphan that passed on the screen.

When they went upstairs to bed, Bridget took longer to check on their two-year-old daughter Chelsea. Ronald watched from the doorway as his wife monitored their daughter's pulse and rearranged her blankets.

Ronald spooned Bridget in bed. Her shoulders were stiff, even after he tried massaging them.

Did you ever see that? she asked.

Ronald smoothed out her blond hair. Yes.

Why didn't you ever tell me?

I saw a lot of horrible things. There were too many to tell.

She didn't respond. He coaxed his hand around her stomach. She patted his arm tentatively.

We can make a donation, Ronald said. Money, supplies, anything you want.

She turned to face him, a small smile on her face. Okay.

For several months, Bridget spent the weekends packing up boxes of diapers and baby formula to ship to needy adoption agencies in Vietnam. But that wasn't enough to satisfy her. From a colleague, Bridget learned about an organization that sent volunteer physicians to Vietnam for two-month humanitarian missions. Ronald supported Bridget's decision to go, even considered taking time off work to go with her. He could act as her guide. But they ultimately decided he should stay behind to take care of Chelsea. They'd never spent more than a week apart since getting married.

A large group of relatives and friends gathered at the airport to say good-bye, tight smiles across their faces, loudly agreeing that what Bridget was doing was admirable and Christian. Ronald knew they were lying, disapproving of a young mother leaving to enter a war zone that had become so unpopular. If Bridget noticed, she didn't say anything. She was always one to do what she thought was right, even if others disagreed. Bridget's parents knew this. They didn't even come to the airport, wishing their daughter good luck over the phone the night before.

Only two, Chelsea didn't understand why she was removed from her grandmother's soft arms so abruptly, and squirmed in protest. Bridget kissed Chelsea's wet cheek and handed her back to Ronald's mother. Then she turned to her husband.

It won't feel like that long, Ronald whispered in her ear. Bridget pressed her forehead into the crook of his shoulder. You'll be back before we even get a chance to miss you.

When she heard the news, her first priority was calling home. Bridget asked Dang, one of the center's employees, to stay on the phone with the international operator and alert her when the call was connected.

They were leaving for America. Vietnam was collapsing, no longer a premonition, but a fact. The adoption agency had been granted permission that morning to evacuate their orphans from Saigon immediately. A plane was waiting for them at the Tan Son Nhut airport. Some of the children found the staff's tears contagious, though their feelings held more confusion and fear than the adults.

As the adults scrambled around the center, frantic with preparations and packing, the children lined around the dining room for their preflight physicals. Bridget knelt on the floor to examine the younger toddlers. Their skin and hair were damp from baths, bodies fresh in clean, new clothes. Bridget playfully tickled them. She assured them their first plane ride would be exciting, not scary.

Dang waved at her from across the room. We got through.

She took the call in Sophie's office, shutting the door behind her. Her hands were shaking as she pressed the phone to her ear.

Hello, she said.

Hi. His voice was faint, but she knew it was Ronald's.

I'm coming home.

Static, the fuzzy echoes of other global conversations, crowded the silence.

Did you hear me? Bridget asked. Hello?

After several seconds, she heard Ronald clear his throat. Yes.

She gave him the necessary details. The agency staff would accompany the orphans out of Saigon. They would change planes in Tokyo and Hawaii and arrive in the States within a few days.

I'll call you when I know the times.

Okay.

So you'll tell my parents?

Sure.

Bridget looked up, suddenly aware she still had more children to examine. There would be time to talk later, all the time they wanted. She'd missed his voice.

I have a surprise, Bridget said. I think you and Chelsea will be very happy with it.

Just come home safe, Bridget.

Okay. She smiled. I'll see you soon.

She returned to the dining room, where the next child in line was Phu, a seven-year-old boy with a harelip. Worry creased between his eyebrows in three soft lines as Bridget checked his eyes and inside his ears. What is it like? he asked once she removed the thermometer, his Vietnamese quiet and shy.

America? Bridget asked.

Phu nodded.

It's safe, Bridget said. With lots of playgrounds.

Phu appeared to consider this. Will we all live together?

I don't think so, Bridget said. You will be living with your new parents. You're going to meet them very soon. Aren't you excited?

He didn't look it, Bridget realized. He didn't understand how lucky he was already to have a set of adoptive parents waiting for him in America. There were still unassigned children at the center who would leave for America unsure of their future homes.

But I can't speak English, Phu said.

You will learn, Bridget said. Like I learned Vietnamese when I came here.

What if I can't?

You will.

But what if I can't? What if my new parents don't like me? What will I do?

His small fingers stretched out the bottom of his new, white shirt. Bridget realized there was nothing she could say to reassure him. Though his home country was falling apart, it was all he knew, and thus, better than an unknown land across the ocean, full of unknown people.

While the children were provided with identification armbands, Bridget ran upstairs to find any stray toddlers who had managed to escape examination. She really wanted to see her boy. He was in the nursery, grouped with the under-three-year-old infants.

Hey, Bridget said, leaning over his crib.

He was sitting up, his eyes wide to the chaos around him. He smiled at her in recognition, lifting one caramel-colored hand to touch her face.

Huan was almost two years old, according to Bridget's examination, when he arrived at the center with a group of other babies from an orphanage in the Mekong Delta. Upon seeing him, she immediately knew he was going to be her son. If only it had happened sooner. She put in the papers for adoption immediately. Though she knew the process took several months, she was sure they'd be in America soon. Bridget was confident that once there, she could take Huan home.

A soft, quick knock on the front door. Ronald looked through the peephole.

Who's there? I don't see anybody.

Daddy, it's me.

Chelsea? Is that you? Where are you?

Down here, Daddy!

Ronald opened the door. Chelsea attacked his legs, wrapping her arms tightly around them.

Were you playing around? she asked as he knelt on the floor to hug her properly.

Yeah, sweetie, I was just playing around.

She grinned at him. Almost five years old, Chelsea's blond pigtails were darkening, showing more streaks of honey brown, the one physical trait she seemed to inherit from Ronald.

Bridget's father, David, approached them, holding Chelsea's backpack and thermos.

Were you good for Grandpa and Grandma last night? Ronald asked.

Chelsea nodded. Can I go play now?

Only for twenty minutes. Then you need to take a bath.

After Chelsea ran upstairs, Ronald turned to David. Can you come in? he asked.

What's the matter? David asked, as they walked into the living room.

Bridget's coming back.

Well, David said, sitting on the couch. We knew this would happen. Damn gooks are going to take Saigon any day now. Did she call you?

Ronald nodded.

Are you going to tell Chelsea?

I'm not sure yet.

Probably shouldn't. Don't want to get the kid's hopes up again.

I really think she's coming back this time.

David shook his head at Ronald sympathetically. I know my daughter, Ronny. And so do you.

When Ronald first met Bridget's parents, they didn't hide the fact that they disliked him. They wondered what a recently discharged army officer could have in common with their young, ambitious, medical student daughter. They were suspicious of his age. They didn't understand why Bridget insisted on getting married right away. Ronald understood their reservations and remained doggedly friendly with them, even when they were rude. Eventually, they grew comfortable with Ronald. Now, after everything, David liked him more than his own daughter.

Where is she going to stay? David asked.

Here, I guess, Ronald said. The house is still in her name.

David stretched his arms out along the back of the couch and scrutinized Ronald with doubtful eyes. Will that be all right with everybody?

Chelsea needs to spend time with her mother, Ronald said. It has to be all right.

Bridget only had one suitcase to pack in the dormitory she lived in behind the center. She'd been preparing for this day for months, slowly trimming down her personal belongings for the impending evacuation. Since the last American troops withdrew in 1973, Bridget knew the southern government could do little against a northern invasion. Once the Communists took over the capital, the U.S. embassy would be forced out, along with all foreign charity workers and volunteers.

Though Sophie had arranged for the Vietnamese staff and their immediate families to come along on the evacuation flight, some of them chose to stay. Bridget couldn't understand this. She tried to talk some sense into Hoa, one of the agency's most loyal employees, who'd decided not to go.

You need to think of your boys, Bridget said. They're not safe here.

Hoa shook her head stubbornly. I can't leave any of my family behind. Hoa's husband and oldest son were in the South Vietnamese army.

Why don't you let us take your boys, then? Bridget suggested. We'll keep them safe. I promise, until you can come to America.

There were tears in Hoa's eyes. It's very generous, but they need to be with me.

You're being selfish. Bridget knew her words were cruel, but they had to be. Hoa didn't understand the reality of the situation.

No, Hoa said firmly. I'm their mother. They're my responsibility.

The buses and escorts arrived early. The police patrolled the crowds trying to push against the center's gates. The children squeezed onto buses, with the older kids propping toddlers on their laps. The babies were put in cribs, boxes, and baskets, and laid out in vans lined with blankets and mats. Two staff members were assigned to each vehicle. They said good-bye to Hoa and the other staff members remaining behind and boarded the vans. Sophie and Bridget took the leading van.

The police jeeps turned on their lights and sirens as the vans and buses started their engines. Despite police escorts, they had trouble driving through the city streets as pedestrians and mopeds weaved recklessly through traffic. Some tripped over the sandbags and barbed wire surrounding the palm-tree-lined medians. On sidewalks, peasant families hunched over straw mats, eating communal bowls of rice. Bridget pressed a palm on the smudged, foggy window. There were still so many people who needed help. But it was time to leave.

Closer to the airport, barbed wire and jeeps cluttered the

streets, with solemn-faced soldiers clinging to their weapons with both hands. The soldiers saluted and waved the long line of vans and buses through security. Inside the wire fence perimeter of the airport, jungle-colored military aircraft spread across the runways. The airport buildings were run-down and unpainted. A large plane took off dangerously close to their vehicles, the noise of its engines deafening.

Soldiers and airport officials wandered around their vans, waving and comparing documents. No one seemed to know who was in charge. With the engines turned off, there was no circulation, allowing the air inside to thicken and bake. Bridget's head felt heavy, her long hair drenched in sweat. She peeled her damp arms off the hot vinyl seat.

Sophie poked her head out of the van and yelled for one of the airport officials.

The babies can't stay cooped up in these vans any longer, she said. It's too hot.

We are waiting for clearance.

That's fine, Bridget said, interrupting. But we're not sitting here. I'm a doctor, and it's my medical opinion that these children will collapse in this heat.

You will have to wait, the official said. Despite what you think, you are not the only ones leaving today. There are other people here more important than your precious bastards.

If one of these children dehydrates and dies, Bridget said, it will be your responsibility.

Sophie nodded in agreement. The official stared at them suspiciously for a moment, turned, and left. Bridget and Sophie peered through the window, watching as he spoke with several other officers. Within minutes, two soldiers blew whistles and gestured for the vans and buses to follow them.

They were directed to the front of a paint-chipped building

surrounded by a thin strip of yellowing grass. An old luxury airport lounge when the French held power, it now stood abandoned off an unused runway. While the children stepped off the buses and stretched, their new clothes dark with perspiration, the staff went to ventilate and clean out the main room of the building. With Huan propped on her hip, Bridget looked over her master list of medications to make sure no one had missed any doses.

Airport personnel were exercising extra caution with their flights. An airport official said there were rumors of sabotage, bombs and weapons targeting any aircraft intending to leave with the country's children. Soldiers were thoroughly searching the airport and adjoining military base.

After feeding the children and changing diapers, the adults, in shifts, took cigarette breaks. Some gathered outside, under the shade of a small awning, watching the planes take off. Bridget stood in the sun, enjoying the faint, warm breeze that drifted through the air.

In a few hours we'll be on one of those, said Steven, squinting at a plane climbing through the sky. Steven was their youngest American volunteer; he had graduated from college the previous year.

Yeah, and you just got here, said Harold, a former freelance journalist from Canada.

Oh, I don't mind, Steven said. I didn't realize how much I missed in America. Just the food, hamburgers, ice cream. And I've only been gone a month. You guys must be dying to get home.

I called my wife this morning, Harold said. I wish I could have seen her reaction.

Steven turned to Bridget. And you must be excited about seeing your daughter.

Bridget nodded.

Three years. Steven shook his head. Wow. I don't know if I could have lasted that long.

I had to, Bridget said. These children's lives are more important to me than hamburgers.

Steven stared at her for a moment and turned to ask Harold about their flight itineraries. Bridget wandered away, alongside the building, the dead, yellow grass crunching beneath her sneakers. She had very little patience for complainers. She'd watched volunteers come and go through the orphanage. The unsure, the apprehensive, could not survive in this environment. They often quit within weeks, sometimes even days. You had to be aggressive to do this kind of work, even egotistical. You had to believe you could do it in the face of anything.

Pollution from the planes tickled her throat, and she coughed several times, attempting to expel the dirty air. Though exhausted, Bridget forced herself to keep walking, unable to stand still. She ran her hand along the wired fence, the rust scraping against her palm.

The problem with downtime was that it allowed the mind to wander and panic over things that were ultimately out of her control. For the last three years, Bridget had operated on little sleep and time, too many people who needed her, so much work to do. It forced her to focus on the immediate, pared priorities down to what she could accomplish at the moment. The work suited her. She couldn't afford to let her mind distract her, especially if the concerns were an ocean away.

During the rare empty pockets of time, she wished her family could understand why she needed to stay in Vietnam for the time being. Bridget remembered one scathing letter from her father, berating her for abandoning her family. He didn't understand. They were safe and secure in America, but these children were not.

When Bridget returned to the airport lounge, she saw a priest standing in front of the adults. The children were looking up at them curiously. The priest was performing a mass marriage ceremony between American and Vietnamese staff members. It was a sham, temporary unions of convenience so that the Vietnamese employees could slide through immigration. Bridget had been relieved when she didn't have to volunteer. Even though the nuptials weren't real, Bridget wanted to cherish the one wedding she had participated in.

Eight years ago, Bridget and Ronald exchanged vows in the backyard of Ronald's family's house. They had a barbecue reception instead of a fancy dinner, a pool volleyball game in lieu of dancing. During the dog days of August, the wedding party toasted the newlyweds with chilled beer bottles. At that moment, a life with Ronald was enough. Their unknown future, the possibilities, thrilled her. At the end of the night, though sunburned and weary, Bridget couldn't stop smiling at her new husband.

In the airport lounge, the priest raised his hands and the odd couples bowed their heads. They signed the papers and returned to work.

Ronald's tour of duty occurred in the early sixties, before the war escalated, when the country still favored it. His work was mainly reconnaissance missions, exploring the countryside, which in many places was just beautiful. He did witness the poverty, but he was sure it was not to the extent Bridget experienced. It seemed unfair that he saw the splendor of Vietnam when he was there to fight, while his wife only saw the suffering, and she was there to help.

The first few weeks away were terribly hard on Bridget. She called as often as she could, with a new complaint about the heat or the food. She'd never had fainting spells before. She was embarrassed about them. Ronald tried to advise her on what to eat, remembering what upset his system when he was in Vietnam, but Bridget's stomach seemed to reject everything.

My body hates this country, Bridget said. Or maybe it just hates me.

You need to give yourself time, Ronald said.

Maybe this was a mistake. I thought I could help.

You are helping.

It doesn't feel like it. How's Chelsea? Can I talk to her?

He'd put their sleepy daughter's ear to the phone and watch Chelsea's smile grow at hearing her mother's voice.

I miss her, Bridget said, after Ronald returned to the phone. I miss both of you.

Ronald cheered her through the homesickness, reminding her she would only be there for two months. He refrained from expressing his biggest concern: the nightly news was predicting the war would soon creep southward. She needed to know he had faith in her. She couldn't know he worried about her safety constantly, that he stayed up at night wondering what was happening between their phone calls.

After the first month, her concerns transferred from herself to the children she cared for. I've never seen babies this emaciated, she said. They're so dehydrated they can't even cry real tears.

She deplored the living conditions of the orphanages, since the majority didn't have on-staff physicians or registered nurses. On alternate calls she rejoiced over prescribing the correct medication for a child's infection or wept over an abandoned newborn's death. Far different from the clinical detachment she maintained working at the children's hospital in Pittsburgh. Yes, she was dealing with more life-and-death situations in Vietnam, but her intense mood swings, contingent upon these children's survival, worried Ronald. It was impossible for Bridget to save them all, but she seemed determined to do so.

A week before her scheduled return, Bridget called Ronald. The agency hadn't found another doctor to replace Bridget when she left. The orphanage wanted her to stay on a few more months.

Did you check with the hospital? Ronald asked.

I don't care about the hospital. The work I do there is not nearly as important as what's being done here. But I care what you think. Is this okay?

Chelsea and I will be fine. But what about you? Do you think you can last there a little longer?

I guess I have to. These children don't have anyone else.

He couldn't ask her to leave. Right now, Bridget needed to help those children.

A week later, there was a profile on Bridget in the *Pittsburgh Gazette*. The reporter had interviewed Bridget over the phone and talked to Ronald, volunteers from the adoption charity, and Bridget's mother. In the article, Ronald spoke of his wife's bravery. He remembered when Bridget once dislocated her shoulder skiing and had to walk two miles in the snow to the nearest ski patrol. The charity volunteers called her a modern saint, selfless and generous. Bridget's mother said she was concerned for her daughter's safety. A picture of Bridget was on the inside page. Her face looked skinnier, bags under her eyes, her hair in a ponytail. Surrounding her were smiling, adoring, Vietnamese children. She held a child in her lap, who touched her face like Chelsea used to. Bridget never looked happier.

In the corner between the restrooms and closet, Sophie set up her office, crouching over a circle of files. She still had a lot of paperwork to sort through before they arrived in America, where adoptive parents and social workers would be waiting and expecting order. Peering at the large piles of manila folders surrounding the director, Bridget wondered where her file was.

Bridget and Thanh reviewed the list of children, which had to be presented in triplicate to immigration before takeoff. They were required to list each orphan with his or her full Vietnamese name and age, a difficult task since most of the children had arrived without birth certificates. They'd resorted to making up middle and last names for the children. While Bridget made sure each name corresponded with the identification tags, Huan played his favorite game of tangling himself between Bridget's legs and trying to wiggle out.

At the front door, a plump, frizzy-haired woman took pictures of some of the sleeping toddlers.

Excuse me, Bridget said, walking up to her. What are you doing?

The woman lowered her thick black camera. Hi, she said brightly, thrusting her right hand between them. My name is Ellen Kelly, I'm a reporter with the Associated Press. I'm doing a story on your trip.

She shook the journalist's hand. I don't know if you're allowed to take photos of the children.

I'm sorry. They just looked so cute sleeping. I'll stop. But would you mind if I asked you some questions?

They sat on a wooden bench outside the building. Across several runways, past the wire perimeter, the concrete turned into rice fields and palm trees. The lush greenery of the landscape contrasted sharply with the smoggy gray of the airport. Huan struggled in Bridget's arms, wanting to crawl on the ground and explore; but it was too hot, and she feared he'd burn himself on the hot tarmac. Ellen balanced a tape recorder and a pad of paper in her hands. Bridget swallowed several times, trying to moisten her scratchy throat. She reminded herself she'd done newspaper interviews before. She could handle this.

Your full name?

Bridget Deborah Andrews.

Hometown?

Pittsburgh, Pennsylvania.

Married?

Bridget hesitated. Yes.

Any children?

I'm sorry. What does this have to do with the story?

Our readers are interested in knowing those Americans who come to Vietnam to do this charity work. It takes a very confident and courageous person. How long have you been in Vietnam?

Almost three years.

That's a long time to be away from your family and friends. How were you able to do it?

Well, Bridget said. I realized that I was needed here. Many of these orphans lack medical attention. I feel I provide an important service.

That's very brave of you.

Bridget couldn't respond. She wasn't sure if the reporter was genuinely giving her a compliment or mocking her. After asking more questions about her personal life, the reporter finally turned to the subject matter.

How many children do we have here?

Bridget looked around. Almost eighty. Small, compared to how many else there are in Vietnam.

A million and a half, with nearly a quarter of them Amerasian?

Yes. Bridget was impressed. Ellen had done her research.

What inspired you to do this?

I saw a story on the news about these orphans, and, as a physician, I wanted to help.

What about the orphans in America?

Bridget stared at the reporter, who was still scribbling in her notebook. Excuse me?

Ellen looked up, her expression direct and confident. There are critics back home who wonder why you're not helping orphans in your own country. How do you respond to that?

I don't know why I have to. Orphans are orphans, no matter where they are. These children are living in a war zone. These Amerasians are children of the U.S. military; they're products of this war.

And you think they'll be better off in America as reminders of such an unpopular war? Wouldn't they benefit from living in their own culture?

Their culture has rejected them. They're outcasts here.

Ellen nodded, seemingly satisfied with her answer. And then:

How do you respond to rumors that this evacuation is a politically motivated publicity stunt to create more sympathy for the war support?

You know, if this publicity stunt means these children are going to be safe, that's fine. Many of these children already have parents waiting for them in America. As far as I'm concerned, they're going home.

But what about the South Vietnamese government's complaints—

A deep, growling explosion startled both women, the impact slamming their backs against the building wall. The air on the runway soon filled with dark, billowing smoke, curling slowly toward thc building.

Huan burst into tears. Bridget stood up, holding him closer to her chest, and squinted through the afternoon haze. On the other side of the wire fence, past the rice paddy Bridget had been admiring before, violent black and orange flames soared to the sky.

The reporter reacted quickly, gathering her items and rushing across the tarmac, straight toward the explosion. But Bridget could only stare.

Several volunteers rushed out and stood next to Bridget and Huan. They shielded their eyes, struggling to see past the smoke. The familiar alarms of fire engines and paramedics and the pulsing of helicopter wings grew steadily louder, until it was all they could hear.

Everyone inside, Sophie said. The children will be scared.

They twisted the blinds closed to alleviate the heat and protect the children. Sophie, Harold, and Steven left for the main terminal to find out what happened. The nurses told the children it was an unscheduled nap time, so they would be plenty rested for their flight. They knew better. Bridget curled on a mat with Huan and several other children. With the blinds closed, they could pretend it was night.

Ronald no longer kept a phone in the bedroom and had to stumble downstairs to answer it. He suspected it was a crank call when the voice on the other line was gasping and crying. After several minutes, Ronald realized it was his mother-in-law, Margaret. She wanted to know if Ronald had heard from Bridget.

Not since this afternoon. She said they were leaving today.

There was a plane crash.

What?

A whole plane of babies. Oh God, it really might be them.

You don't know?

A few minutes ago, David had received a call from a reporter saying that one of the evacuation flights from Saigon had crashed. It wasn't clear what adoption agencies were on board, since several Babylift flights were scheduled to leave the same day. On the news radio, they were reporting growing numbers of casualties. The reporter wanted to know how they felt about their daughter dying in the crash.

All Ronald could hear for several minutes was Margaret sobbing. When she finally took a breath, he invited them over.

I knew it was too good to be true, Margaret said. They sat in the living room. Just when my baby's ready to come home, those horrible Orientals sabotage her plane. She buried her face in her hands.

We don't know if she was on that flight, Ronald said. We don't know anything.

She brought this on herself, David said.

C'mon, Ronald said.

How can you be so cruel? Margaret asked.

I told her this could happen, David said. She knew better but she didn't care.

Lower your voice, Margaret said. Chelsea's sleeping.

It's true, David said, his voice growing louder. I'm sorry, honey, but she wanted to bring gook babies into our country, and now she's getting punished for it.

Hey, Ronald said, looking up. That's enough.

Why are you getting mad at me? David asked.

Those babies didn't deserve to die. And neither does Bridget.

She knew the risks, David said. Did you hang around Vietnam after your tour ended? No. You told me what it was like. You couldn't wait to leave.

Bridget went to Vietnam because she wanted to help people. That's not a crime. She was trying to do a good thing.

But how did she do it? By leaving her family. She left all of us, for strangers.

Ronald retreated to the kitchen to make some tea for Margaret. He sat at the kitchen table instead. He realized how foolish it was not to entertain this possibility. He'd spent so much of the last two years angry at Bridget for leaving. He finally had to admit that their marriage was over. It didn't occur to him that Bridget could die. That he would never see her again. He thought of their daughter upstairs. Chelsea might have to grow up without her mother.

The C-5A Galaxy, the largest military aircraft in the U.S. Air Force, destined for the Philippines with approximately 330 passengers, most of them children, had crashed into a rice paddy forty-two minutes after takeoff, after apparently trying to return for an emergency landing. Rescue workers found the plane in four pieces, both of the wings broken off, infant clothes and toys scattered across the rice field. All rescued passengers were taken to nearby hospitals. Casualty and injury information was not yet available, but from outside their building, they could see rescue workers hauling away more body bags than survivors. Normally the stoic one, Sophie couldn't finish delivering the news to her staff. Harold held her hand, while Thanh smoothed Sophie's frazzled silver hair.

Why would anyone want to kill babies? Sophie asked.

Outgoing flights were suspended. Planes sat idle on the runway. Ground control members squatted together on tarmac, their unlit flares uselessly hanging from their rear pants pockets. Steven and Harold made several trips to the main terminal to find updated information on their flight status.

Eventually, one of the pilots for their flight stopped by the building. He sat on the edge of his chair, his back rigid, maintaining more eye contact with his watch than Sophie or anyone else.

We would still like to fly out this evening, the pilot said. We've searched the aircraft thoroughly and will continue to do so until takeoff. The army has assured us that our plane will be closely surveilled and protected until we're safely in the air.

Didn't the army try to protect that other plane? Sophie asked.

We don't know what caused that accident. We have no idea. It might have been sabotage, but it could have also been a malfunction in the plane. Our aircraft has passed a meticulous inspection. If you still want to leave, we can. In my opinion, the sooner we leave, the better.

You don't want to do this, do you? Bridget asked. He was

probably used to more important missions, like flying into battle and rescuing ground soldiers. Perhaps he considered transporting children beneath him.

I take all my orders seriously, ma'am, he said, appearing unfazed by her question. My crew and I have a lot of work to do before we leave, so I should go now to help them.

We should wait, Bridget said, once the pilot left. We can leave tomorrow after they find out what caused that crash.

But the pilot said it was safe, Harold said. If they feel comfortable flying, then maybe we should, too.

We just watched a planeful of children go down, Bridget said. How can you want to get on a plane today?

That provoked many to weigh in with their opinions, mostly the Americans. The Vietnamese staff, many of whom had never flown before, listened, their confusion over the split opinion clouding their faces. People shouted over each other to be heard.

It's our only way out of this country. We should do it before it's too late.

This could have been a warning. We can't just ignore it.

Or it might not. We shouldn't let it scare us.

What about the children? Do you want to be responsible for their deaths?

Do you want to be responsible if we stay?

We don't know what happened, Sophie said. They quieted when the director spoke, since her opinion mattered. The danger of staying here is still real. That's why we wanted to leave today.

But there might be more danger up there, Bridget said.

You know, for a doctor, you don't have much logic, Harold said. He glared at Bridget savagely. If you don't want to leave, fine, but some of us want to go home.

Bridget turned to look at Sophie. She had to be sensible and agree with her. The director's arms were crossed, and she chewed on her lip.

It's too risky, Bridget said to Sophie. It's foolish.

Hon, Sophie said. She sounded tired. Our whole time here has been risky.

They spent another half hour debating, but Bridget knew Sophie had made up her mind. They would depart, even though from the airport lounge, they could still see rescue workers removing bodies from the crash site.

Their conversations only grew worse with time. Bridget was upset if Chelsea was asleep when she called, accusing Ronald of allowing their daughter to forget her. He reminded her that by returning home she could fix that. She told him he never listened to her anymore, didn't care about the things she was trying to accomplish. If he did, he wouldn't make her feel so guilty.

You don't understand, Bridget said, during one of their arguments. Do you know how many babies here are Amerasian?

What does that matter? Ronald asked.

Are you kidding? These children are here because of American soldiers who couldn't keep their pants on.

Are you blaming me?

So you never slept with anyone while you were in Vietnam?

They were mean to each other. They'd never been mean before. He told her the bravery he once admired in her was really callousness. Since she didn't allow herself to feel pain and fear, she couldn't comprehend them in those she was supposed to love. But deep down, she was terrified, only she refused to admit it.

You don't want to see what you've done to me and Chelsea, Ronald said. You'd rather live in a battlefield.

That's not true, Bridget said.

Then come home. Fix this.

Stop being so selfish, Ronald. I can't.

Eighteen months after Bridget's departure, Ronald ordered her to come back. She refused. The next week, Ronald met with a lawyer to draw up official separation papers.

She called him once she received the legal documents. Her voice was trembling.

Why are you acting surprised? he asked. You knew this was the next step.

I'm coming back. She couldn't even say it convincingly anymore.

No, Ronald said. Not to us.

In the army, Ronald had been trained and prepared for the political and social landscape of Vietnam. A six-month boot camp that included language and cultural training. Even then, the culture shock was dramatic. Bridget received no such preparation. She was thrown into the chaos, no chance to adjust, deluged by children who expected her help. She endured the danger of living in a war-torn country so she could treat these orphans. While Ronald didn't agree with everything she did, her motives were generous. All her hard work to rescue those children, and now they could all be dead.

As departure time loomed, the adults occupied themselves with preparation details and the children played games. Some employees were hesitant to feed the infants after the earlier diarrhea scare, but Bridget inspected a case of formula she had packed herself and approved its use.

Everyone was jittery to leave. The metal roof retained most of the day's heat, lingering smells of urine and spoiled milk pervading the room. The airport had dispatched security around their building, but Bridget could still hear the sirens and skidding tires as more bodies were transported to the hospital.

Bridget stepped outside for a cigarette. The sun was setting, the crash site blurry in the rosy haze. The authorities had sectioned off the rice paddy, the blue-and-red lights of the paramedics and fire engines still flashing, though slower than before. What those children must have been feeling during takeoff. So thrilled for their first plane trip, and excited about America. They hardly got off the ground.

When Bridget returned inside, Sophie approached her.

We need to talk about Huan, Sophie said.

What's wrong? Bridget asked. She'd left him sleeping on the mat. Bridget looked over to see he was still there, curled in the fetal position.

He's fine, Sophie said. But I wanted to talk to you about your adoption application. There's a problem with his papers.

What?

The adoption hasn't been approved. At least not yet. You can't take him home with you right away. There's a couple in California who thinks Huan is theirs.

Bridget stared at her. How did that happen?

Your application was suspended for further review, so they kept Huan on the available adoption list.

What are they reviewing?

Sophie hesitated. There are some details the board didn't understand.

Just tell me what it is, so I can fix it.

Your separation—

Single parents are allowed to adopt—

But your daughter. Sophie cleared her throat. They don't understand why you'd want to adopt another child when you haven't seen your own in three years.

Bridget planted her feet solidly on the floor. The gravity of those words traveled through her spine. Ronald, Chelsea, her career, three years of her life. All of this wasted.

But, Bridget struggled to speak. You know why I stayed in Vietnam.

I do, Sophie said. And I sympathize completely. Once we're in America, I will explain your position and hopefully, this will all be figured out. I'm sorry. You know communication with the main office is very bad. On paper, they don't know like I do that you'll make a good parent.

Why didn't you tell me this before? Bridget could hardly breathe.

I assure you, Bridget, you will be able to adopt a child.

Huan, Bridget said. I want Huan.

I know, Sophie said, rubbing her arm soothingly. I'm so sorry, hon, I wish I could have told you earlier, but really, we can't do anything until we're in America. I promise you this will work itself out very soon.

When Bridget picked him up from his nap, he molded his body to her so naturally, offering a little yawn and glancing around the room.

Hey, sweetie, she said. Huan tucked his face between her neck and shoulder and sighed peacefully.

He had entered her life at the perfect time, her angel, the affirmation she needed to remember why she'd come to Vietnam. Ronald had just mailed her the official separation papers. She never thought he'd go this far. He wouldn't take her calls unless they were talking about Chelsea. If she tried to bring up their marriage, he'd hang up. Bridget had begun to wonder if she'd made a terrible mistake. But then Huan appeared. One of the orphans brought over from the Delta. Hoa was bathing him after his long car ride when Bridget came over to examine him. Huan smiled at Bridget, wet, fresh, and clean.

You're mine, aren't you? She patted his diaper to feel if it was still dry. His hand curled comfortably on her shoulder. You are.

Ronald walked outside to the backyard, where David and Margaret sat reading on the deck. Chelsea played in the sandbox, trying to scoop sand with a broken plastic shovel.

Bridget wasn't on the plane, Ronald said. It was a different agency.

Margaret stared at him. Are they sure?

Yes.

Where's Bridget?

Her agency is scheduled for a later flight. That's all we know for now.

She's alive, Margaret said, closing her eyes. She's coming back. David took his wife's hand into his. They smiled at each other, relieved.

Ronald walked up to the sandbox. What are you making?

A bed.

What about your bed upstairs?

No, for the ants.

Oh. Ronald knelt on the grass, one hand on the edge of the sandbox. Hey, sweetie, I have some news.

Chelsea continued digging. Yeah?

Your mommy's coming home.

Really? Chelsea didn't look up.

Yes. She'll be back in a few days. She told me to tell you she's very excited about seeing you and that she loves you very much.

Chelsea glanced up, her green eyes so big and unblinking. Is she going to stay?

Yes.

That's nice. She went back to shoveling.

Ronald patted her daughter's silky hair. She was young, unspoiled by years. She didn't know what abandonment, rejection, or bitterness felt like beyond her world of sandboxes and playgrounds. She ultimately wouldn't remember the years her mother was gone. Ronald was grateful for that. Bridget should be, too. She still had a chance to make it up to Chelsea. She could still be a good mother.

Though the sun had set, the black tarmac and aluminum stairs to the plane radiated the day's heat through their shoes. The staff formed a receiving line for the infants, passing each crib, box, and basket along until all had boarded. They smiled at the other passengers, another agency from the other side of Saigon. Some recognized each other from maternity wards and the immigration office, and waved.

The military plane was vast, even for two orphanages. While there were several long rows of tan canvas seats in the front, the main cabin was empty, the large floor covered in army green blankets and pillows. The older children in the front seats curiously stared out the Plexiglas windows, waving to ground control crew inspecting the plane.

They strapped the babies in with long, thick seat belts that draped over five cribs each. Over the children's crying and questions, the flight crew shouted their instructions. Airport officials arrived, once again searching all the plane's compartments and under the seats. They detected nothing, and the officials nodded their approval.

Three immigration officers boarded for final inspection. Harold and Dang motioned for the older boys to slump low in their seats.

The officers took their time wandering down the aisles, suspiciously examining each child's face and matching it to the corresponding name and birth date. Bridget stared ahead as the officers passed her. Immigration had the authority to yank any child they wanted off the plane. If that happened, it was unclear what would happen to those children. Probably sent back to another orphanage. Or worse for the boys, drafted.

One of the officers stopped for a long time in front of Nghi, a twelve-year-old boy whose identification claimed he was nine. Nghi stared at the floor.

The officer crossed her arms. Stand up, she barked.

Nghi looked over to Harold, seated next to him.

What seems to be the problem? Harold asked in Vietnamese.

This boy seems very mature for a nine-year-old, the officer said, still glaring at Nghi. Stand up, boy, so I can get a closer look at you.

Still staring at Harold, Nghi stood, trembling.

The officer squinted at the boy and looked again at the identification papers, shaking her head.

Excuse me, someone said loudly. The pilot stood at the cockpit door, glaring into the main cabin. You're holding up our departure.

We are still clearing the children, the officer said in English. It is procedure.

I don't care, the pilot said. He strode down the aisle to where the officer and Nghi stood. Ground control is ordering us on the runway now. We're already an hour late.

You are still in Saigon. This plane must still abide by government regulations.

The U.S. military is expecting us in Tokyo in several hours. This plane is under orders to abide by their regulations.

She looked to her fellow immigration officers. A few silent nods between them. The officer straightened her back, and, without looking at the pilot, muttered they'd finish their inspection shortly. The immigration officers left soon after, hurriedly granting clearance and disembarking the plane without speaking another word to the staff.

Thank you, Sophie said to the pilot, as the children stared at him in awe.

The pilots turned the aircraft to power down the runway. The passengers were warned that military planes were not insulated and cupped their ears against the overwhelming engine noise. The airplane lifted off, climbing so steeply into the air, they were almost vertical. The aircraft maintained maximum speed, wary of potential ground fire.

Bridget held Huan closely to her, nuzzling his dark, curly hair. At every bump of turbulence, she caught her breath. She imagined Chelsea, her family, Ronald, all these people she'd taken for granted, that she'd see again. And I will, she reminded herself. It's okay, it's okay, it's okay.

The plane leveled off, and the passengers looked around, exchanging smiles of relief. When the pilot announced they'd reached a safe altitude, the adults gathered the children around the cabin windows to say good-bye. From above, Vietnam appeared a cloud of dark foliage sprinkled with tiny lights. Sparse fires, which might have frightened them on the ground, now seemed luminous. The sea looked silky and clean in the moonlight.

While Bridget glanced briefly out the window, her attention remained on the children. Some of them began to cry, burying their wet faces in their arms. The realization that she would not see them every day as she had for so long suddenly struck her. She held Huan closer to her and returned to their seat.

He was a good-traveling toddler, not like some of the other infants, who were already crying from the change in cabin pressure. Huan's face maintained its serene expression, smiling occasionally to Bridget, before drifting off to sleep.

Their flight was destined for Tokyo. From there, they'd take a flight to Hawaii. Then another to the mainland. Within a few days, they'd be home.

Then, Bridget could fix everything. All the things she'd put on hold, her family, her career, it was not too late. Sophie would work out the adoption paperwork, allowing Huan to come home. She'd find another child for that couple in California to adopt.

Bridget would talk to the hospital about returning to work, resuming her regular rounds at the pediatrics ward. Or she didn't have to. Perhaps she could talk to colleagues who worked in the free clinics downtown. Maybe look into opportunities in emergency care.

Chelsea would finally meet her younger brother. Bridget would take her daughter's hand and place it into Huan's, forging their connection. Chelsea would teach Huan to speak English, and they would protect and support each other like siblings should. She'd finally understand why her mother had to stay away for so long.

In time, perhaps Ronald would, too. Huan needed a father. How could he look into this beautiful face and refuse? Their problems stemmed from their distance. If Bridget could talk to Ronald face-to-face, she could convince him of the things she couldn't over the telephone. He'd realize he still loved her. They could be a family again, a bigger, more complete family.

She'd make them see. They could love each other. They'd be happy. They would appreciate for the rest of their lives the sacrifices that Bridget had made for them, realize she'd been right all along.

MOTHERLAND

THE FIRST IMPRESSION: GAZING, gawking, analysis of the site and its surroundings, discussion on whether it lives up to photographs from history books and brochures. Nods, murmurs, and smiles of recognition. It seems bigger. No, smaller. Opinions vary.

Then the historical context: tour guide Leah in her red visor and matching "Vietnam Specialist" T-shirt, motioning for them to keep up with her.

The Reunification Palace has gone through many transformations during the different political regimes in Vietnam, Leah says, her hand sweeping over her head for effect.

Once the home of the French governor, it is best known as the former central headquarters of the South Vietnamese government. The palace has survived several attacks and renovations through the years and now stands as a museum for us.

Members of the tour consider her their cultural ambassador, eagerly absorbing every word, since Leah has been leading tours in Southeast Asia for almost five years. She says without irony that she considers herself an honorary Vietnamese, to which her travelers, most of whom are white, nod approvingly.

While the palace, with its modern architecture and beautifully manicured gardens and fountains, is impressive, Huan is distracted by the activity surrounding it. On the main boulevard leading to the palace, mopeds and cars noisily tangle in five-lane rush hour. In the gardens around the palace, other tour groups snap pictures of the landmark, while pushcart vendors in conical hats and slippers creep around them, hoping to lure customers with their hot pastries and roasting meats.

Visual recordings come next and usually last the longest. Cameras and camcorders, of various sizes and qualities, emerge frantically once Leah steps out of the way. Postcardlike shots of the site, zoom in and out, then individual photos, and, finally, the group picture, which never takes less than ten minutes to organize.

All right, everyone, Leah yells, squinting behind the company camera. There is an option after the trip to purchase her professional-quality photographs. Get real close. We're one big family, right?

Huan must resist the urge every time to flee the mass photo op, wary of squeezing into another photograph with all those red shirts. But his mother insists. Gwen's eyes plead with him when he tries to edge away, and the dutiful son must acquiesce. He stands next to his old friend Mai, who rests her head against his shoulder. She, too, is tired of the group atmosphere, but they know it is ending soon, at least for today.

They've been sightseeing all morning: the former U.S. embassy, the Notre Dame Cathedral, the Old Post Office, and the Remnants of War Museum. Individually interesting, but packaged in one day, exhausting. The next stop is the Binh Tay market, where Leah promises brief commentary and ample leisure time to wander.

Fifteen minutes are allotted for souvenirs while Leah flags down their motor coach. She instructs them to remain inside the palace garden, so that no one is left behind. She is always worried about losing people.

Do you want something? Gwen asks. The group is dispersing to various gift stands along the plaza, Mai already waiting in line at a dessert vendor. Although Huan's mother already has a large tote bag full of embroideries, a conical hat, and a miniature bronze Buddha statue, she is ready to hunt for more.

No, Huan says. I'm fine. His only purchases so far are postcards to send back to a few coworkers and friends.

Don't you want to come browse with me?

I'm tired, Mom. You go ahead. I'll wait for you here.

Okay. I'll look, and if I find something you might like—

Go, Mom. The bus will be here soon.

She leaves her tote bag with Huan and hustles to the nearest souvenir vendor. Ho Chi Minh City is a land of bargains, anything and everything on sale, an ideal match for Huan's mother, an avid shopper. Yesterday, Gwen was throwing up in the hotel bathroom all afternoon from a dubious rice pudding purchased from a sidewalk peddler. Today, fully recovered, she happily haggles with a vendor over a plastic replica of the palace.

Huan feels a tug on his pant leg. He peers over his sunglasses to the impediment.

A small boy grins a toothless smile, holding a stained cardboard box full of crumpled cigarette boxes, candy, and soda cans. He wears only shorts and rubber sandals. He bumps his merchandise against Huan's thigh. You buy now, suh.

Huan shakes his head.

C'mon. You rich American. Lots of dollahs.

He doesn't smile like he had this morning, when these child peddlers were still new and endearing. Their relentless pursuit and broken, cackling English have gnawed through his patience. Leah's advice is to avoid eye contact with tenacious vendors and beggars, and they will eventually move on. But Huan tries a different tactic, looking directly at the boy, hoping to intimidate him away permanently.

The stare-off lasts several minutes, the boy beaming and Huan scowling. The child thinks it's some kind of game with a prize at the end. Huan grows suspicious that the boy's patience can be greater than his own.

Have you made a friend? Gwen asks, quickly snapping a picture of the two.

Mom, don't, Huan says, as his mother slips the boy a Vietnamese coin piece, but it is too late. The child squeals victoriously and scampers off.

Oh, it's all right.

You've made yourself a target. Now they'll be chasing us down all afternoon.

You're exaggerating.

I'm not. He's going to tell all his friends to look for the American red-haired lady in the red T-shirt. She's giving away money.

Does somebody need a nap?

Mom.

Sweetie, his mother says, squeezing his shoulder. Relax. We're here to enjoy ourselves.

She is determined to do this. Traveling, especially in groups, is much more her thing than Huan's. On their first day, she quickly learns the names, occupations, and home states of all their fellow travelers. In exchange, they know all about Gwen and her Amerasian son's trip to Vietnam, a belated quest to discover his roots, visit the Saigon orphanage he once lived in. She divulges this story to anyone who asks, so proud of Huan's decision to learn more about his native country, something she has encouraged his whole life.

Huan realizes this must come out sooner or later. It is obvious that he and his mother are not biologically related: she, a chubby Caucasian redhead, and he, a lanky half-black, half-Vietnamese with fuzzy black hair. Gwen's enduring strategy to combat raised eyebrows and sneers is to explain their situation frankly: she and her husband adopted Huan once he arrived in America with the Operation Babylift evacuation. The way she gushes over her miraculous family and beautiful son, even the most cynical keep their opinions to themselves.

To her credit, Gwen doesn't mention, not even once to their tour companions, that she isn't supposed to be on this trip. That she is taking the place of Emily, who originally suggested this vacation to Huan for their three-year anniversary. She thought it would be fun to explore his past. Huan didn't even want to go after their breakup, but since they didn't think to buy travel insurance, his mother convinced him not to waste such a lovely trip. She even called his friend Mai, who was teaching in Japan for the year, and persuaded her to meet up with them in Vietnam. Gwen said she was doing this for Huan. It will be good for him to get away and appreciate what he does have, which is so much. His mother tries to see the best in everything and, especially now, is determined to pass this trait down to her son.

The Binh Tay Market is in the Cholon district, a half hour's drive away, so the travelers use the downtime to rest in their tinted, air-conditioned motor coach. There are enough seats for everyone to take two and lie down, but Huan's mother likes for them to sit together. They are on vacation.

The bus is quiet. They are normally a noisy, awkward band of travelers: a mix created solely by coincidental vacation times. They are mostly families, some with small children. One family is Vietnamese, the Vus, who immigrated to America shortly after the Fall and are returning for their first visit. There's a senior couple, the Lewises, who are spending their retirement savings to see the world. There are three U.S. war veteran buddies who never seem embarrassed by their prolific dropping of words like *gooks* and *'Nam.* The old men stare at Huan when they think he's not looking, almost tempting Huan to ask if they left behind their own bastard child in Vietnam.

Mai sits across from them, napping. Her long black hair fans across the cushioned seat, reminding him briefly of Emily. He hasn't seen Mai in a few years and not regularly since high school. She seems comfortable in Vietnam, not complaining like the other tourists of the heat and humidity, probably because she's lived in Asia for the past year.

After college, Mai left for graduate school in England. Then a consulting job in Beijing. Now teaching English in Japan. She is living with a fellow teacher, a Canadian named Gordon, whom Huan has never met.

Too bad, Gwen later says, privately to Huan. She's become so pretty since high school. Good teeth.

Mom. Don't start.

I'm not saying anything. Leah is rather charming, don't you think? I know you don't usually date Caucasian girls, but she seems worldly. Fluent in three languages.

Gwen claims she wants him to date regardless of color, but he knows she is worried that he has never brought home a white girl. His last few girlfriends, including Emily, were Asian. She wants to know why her race is being unilaterally rejected.

Out the window, pink dust filters through the air, illuminating the abandoned colonial French mansions along the wide boulevards. The mopeds, cyclos, and pedestrians around their bus hustle past these ghosts, obsolete remnants of a forgotten foreign invader. The focus is on the bright gold pagoda, the center of the market, leading into hundreds of wooden vendor stalls. Twinkle lights, stuffed animals, and dangling clumps of neon rubber sandals decorate the market's tarp ceilings.

Under the pagoda, Huan's mother eyes him warily. I suppose you want to go off on your own now.

Mom, I love you.

Forget him, Mai says, leaning onto Gwen. He'll just get in the way of shopping. Huan's mother smiles. She has always liked Mai.

Fine, Gwen says. Do you want to meet us for dinner then?

Sure.

Should we set up a meeting place?

I'll just find you.

As he wanders through the stands, Huan realizes there is no farmers' market like this in America. People bump against him, the locals, who are there to do business. Different languages barter and negotiate. Vietnamese, Chinese, Russian. In the livestock section, customers bend over wire cages, poking the live ducks, chickens, and pigs inside. Behind wooden tables soaked dark with blood, butchers prepare fresh meat for customers.

He walks through the aisles, stopping occasionally to watch and listen to exchanges between peddlers and patrons. Sometimes Huan believes if he listens carefully, he will understand the language. At a chicken stall where a woman is plucking a fresh kill, a policeman stares pointedly at Huan. He is wearing a tattered olive green uniform and muddy black boots. A black nightstick and a clunky archaic pistol are prominently displayed on his plastic belt. The cop has to be at least a foot shorter than Huan.

Huan smiles, unsure what else to do. When the policeman only glares, Huan casually turns around, shoving his hands deep in his pockets, and walks away. A few minutes later, he notices the same policeman peering at him from behind a pile of bananas. Huan doesn't stop at any of the stands anymore, the cop only a few paces behind him. Huan pretends not to see him and continues walking, until reaching the edge of the market, then turns around, and walks again.

Twenty minutes of this and the policeman finally approaches him. One hand clenching his nightstick, jaw locked, he barks something at Huan.

Huan shakes his head. I don't understand.

This seems to infuriate the cop even more. He stalks in a circle around Huan, muttering. Huan looks around for the nearest merchant to intercede, but they all avoid eye contact, refusing to get involved. He broadens his circle for help, spotting Mai at a vegetable stall in another aisle. His mother isn't with her.

Mai! Huan yells. The policeman jumps back at this outburst. Embarrassed, the cop begins shouting and jabbing his finger at Huan's chest. His other hand nervously fumbles for the whistle around his neck. Huan realizes if other cops are called in, he will be in more trouble.

Mai walks up to them, carrying a small sack of mangoes. She interrupts the cop's railing, says something in Vietnamese, and the policeman quickly turns his anger on her. They stand eye to eye. She doesn't raise her voice, but she doesn't back down. She listens to what he says and responds calmly. Then she looks over to Huan.

Take your hands out.

What? The cop returns his attention to him.

He thinks you're hiding something in your pockets, Mai says. Show him you're not.

Huan obeys, making a big show of waving his hands in the air.

The policeman huffs another order.

Mai bites her lip and looks at Huan. He wants to pat you down.

Are you kidding?

He thinks you stole something. Just let him do it.

By then, a curious crowd has gathered. Teenage girls, old men, tourists with cameras. Trouble happening to other people is always interesting. Huan hopes his mother is far away in another section of the market. Once Huan nods, granting permission, the cop nearly jumps him, quickly slapping into Huan's arms, legs, and midsection. Huan stares at the ground, trying to control his breathing, attempting to expel his growing rage.

The cop looks triumphant afterward, the humiliation complete. After releasing Huan, he nods, wags his finger at them, and walks off. The audience disperses.

Mai walks up to him. You okay?

Huan looks at her. I want to leave.

They go to the deli section, where faded plastic tables and chairs lie strewn around for weary customers. Mai buys them a plate of pâté chauds, golden flaky pastry shells with spicy meatball middles. They eat them in silence.

It's not fair, Huan finally says.

Yeah, Mai says.

It's bullshit. Did you get that guy's name?

What for?

I'm going to complain.

Mai looks around the market and back at him. To whom?

The police chief, the American embassy, Leah. Someone.

What were you expecting? For everyone to be nice to you?

I didn't expect to be harassed.

This is Vietnam. If they can tell you're at least part-Vietnamese, they're going to have issues with you. I've been dealing with it, too. If you want courtesy for the rest of the trip, go stand next to Leah.

It's different for me.

It's not just you, Mai says. The authorities hate overseas Vietnamese. They think we're rude and arrogant to come back home, throw money around, and expect to be treated like royalty.

I'm not acting like that.

No. They don't know you. So don't take it personally.

He doesn't know why he is. He has experienced discrimination before, plenty of it in America, though his parents did their best to shield him from it. But it bothers him that the Vietnamese are looking down at him, angry at him. They want to show him how un-Vietnamese he is. Well, he knows that. He always has.

As he tries to relax, Huan focuses on his calm, patient companion. Hey, he says, patting her hand. Thanks. He realizes it's a little strange to have Mai, little Mai, rescuing him. Two years older, Huan remembers how nervous and awkward Mai was in high school, how she always sought him out for advice. She has matured during their years apart. She's grown up.

She pats him back. You're welcome.

Where's my mom?

She's standing in line to see a fortune-teller.

A scam.

No, just fun. It's cheap, anyway.

Did she talk to you?

Mai hesitates, then smiles her answer.

I'm sorry, Huan says, staring at his food. She doesn't know when to shut up.

She's worried about you.

This isn't the first time I've been dumped.

I know it's not about Emily.

I don't know what I'm doing here, Huan says. This trip was never my idea. First, it was Emily's, and now my mom's.

Mai looks down at the table. But it's a good idea. So what if it isn't yours?

I'm glad you're here.

Me too.

It's been years, Mai. Are you ever planning on coming back to America?

Sure I am. She takes a bite of pastry and fastidiously wipes her mouth with a napkin. Huan decides not to press her on when.

She tells him more about her classes in Japan and her boyfriend Gordon. He tells her about the new responsibilities at his job and how much work he'll have on his desk once he returns. They reminisce about old high school and college friends. She laughs for the first time on their vacation, a reminder of the old Mai.

What are you doing tomorrow morning? Huan asks.

Why?

We're not going to the tunnels until the afternoon. My mom and I are visiting the nursery center that handled my adoption.

Her face doesn't change at all, and Huan suddenly remembers. Mai is an orphan, too.

If you're busy, it's okay. He feels terrible. How can he forget? Mai grew up in foster homes her whole life. Sometimes she spent college breaks at his family's house.

I'm not, Mai finally says. I'll come.

Okay, Huan says. Thanks. Embarrassed, he looks away, into the crowded market, everywhere heads full of smooth, black hair.

The Children of Mary's Adoption Center is located in an old government building on the western side of District One. The morning traffic on the main boulevard in front of the center is heavy and noisy, and the children are instructed to stay within the building's gates at all times.

In the courtyard, young orphans bustle around Huan's mother. They coo at Gwen with outstretched hands, softly chanting the English word *please* over and over. She smiles at them, struggling with a plastic trash bag in her arms, and dramatically hands each child a stuffed animal, rubber ball, or plastic toy.

When one of the little girls gives his mother a kiss, Huan turns around and heads back inside. He remembers the argument he had with his mother before leaving for Vietnam, when he discovered half her luggage space devoted to these toys. She couldn't understand why he was so angry about the gifts.

These children don't have anything, Huan. What's wrong with giving if we can?

He couldn't bring himself to tell her. The toys would be played with for a few days, but they'd eventually get dirty, break, get thrown away, and the orphans would still be destitute. They didn't need this kind of charity.

He finds Mai in the hallway, looking at photographs of children on the wall. Huan walks up behind her.

Are you looking for her? he asks. Mai's childhood friend Kim was also on the Babylift. Huan never knew her very well, except that she always seemed angry, blaming the bad things that happened in her life on everyone else, often Mai.

Mai nods sheepishly. I don't even know which adoption agency she left from.

Too bad she couldn't come.

She's too busy with her kids and work. Besides, I don't think she would've anyway.

Why not?

Mai pauses for a moment. I think she might hate Vietnam more than she hates America.

Huan can understand that. He wonders if it is one of the few things he and Kim would ever agree on.

Do you ever talk to the Reynoldses anymore? Huan asks.

We write. Christmas cards, birthdays.

No plans to visit?

Mai shakes her head. Not right now. I'm busy, they're busy. They have a new foster child. He's only seven.

They walk along the halls, scrutinizing each picture. Mai slowly wanders ahead of him. Huan hangs back, remembering that Mai doesn't like people watching over her shoulder. She couldn't stand other people looking at the same picture as she at museums. She prefers observing alone.

Huan is grateful that Mai decided to come today. Their cyclo driver got lost twice, raising suspicions that he was trying to pad his fare. Mai sharply threatened him in Vietnamese. A few minutes and two turns later, they arrived at the center.

Eight years ago, the Vietnamese government granted permission for the adoption center to reopen in Ho Chi Minh

City. The facilities look spare, but well maintained, with a fresh coat of paint on the building's exterior and vibrant potted plants in each room. The staff and children seem happy. The orphans stare unabashedly at Huan, recognizing his mixed heritage and that he was once like them. But he isn't. These children are pure Vietnamese.

There are no more Amerasian children, the despised products of American military men and Vietnamese woman finally aborting with the war's end. No, those bastards are grown. Some gone, but not all. Huan realizes he should be more worried about other Amerasians in Vietnam than anyone else. The Amerasians who were left behind have good reason to hate Huan. They had to bear the brunt of a country's devastation and poverty. Huan searches for them in the streets of Ho Chi Minh City, but he hasn't spotted any yet. Perhaps they have learned to fade into the scenery, granting the country's wish just to disappear. The children of the dust mercifully dissipated, the last bitter reminders of a hated war.

Huan feels a tickle on his elbow. Sophie, the center's founder and president, smiles at him. A bone-thin, white-haired American in her seventies, she looks at him like Gwen does, with naïve, hopeless affection. He is getting this a lot today, his status of Babylift orphan suddenly elevating him to Christ child. Sophie was on the same evacuation flight with Huan. She is the one who placed him in Gwen's arms twenty-six years ago.

Thanks again for taking the time to meet with us, Huan says.

Oh it's my pleasure, hon. I always enjoy seeing my babies all grown-up and successful.

Well, I don't know about that.

Oh, hush. She shakes her head at him. So many people loved you, Huan, so many wanted you for their own. I remember.

Huan smiles wanly. She probably says this to every orphan.

Brunch is ready, Sophie says, looking around. Where's your mother?

She's still giving away her toys.

She is such a generous soul, Sophie says, shaking her head. You are so lucky to have her.

Brunch is set up on the patio, tame American cuisine of sandwiches and salads, which Gwen is grateful for.

Not that I don't love all the new, exotic things we're trying here, but I do miss plain, good American food. Am I right?

Sophie and the other staff at the table smile at her. Huan looks over at Mai, whose face appears carefully blank.

They have mementos to share. Sophie passes around photo albums taken during the Babylift, and in those washed-out black-and-white pictures, they try to distinguish Huan from crowds of little faces. There is only one individual photograph of Huan, which Gwen already has a copy of back home. His identification picture, full name Huan Anh Cung, scrawled on a sheet of paper and held in front of his gaunt, confused face.

The admittance and medical records are next. In a thick, faded green book on pages that record many other orphans' lives, they locate Huan's information. He stayed in Sophie's adoption center for nine months before the Babylift evacuation. His biological parents are listed as unknown. He was named by the nuns at the orphanage where he was abandoned. His medical records indicate he suffered from bronchitis, ear infections, and boils.

None of this is new. Huan's mother requested his background information from the adoption center long ago. But he nods and smiles when he is supposed to, because he knows they are all watching him, expecting gratitude and humility.

This information would have been more interesting for Emily. She was always curious about his vague heritage and couldn't understand why he wasn't, too. Emily was not adopted. Born to Korean immigrant parents, she was close to them and her extended family of cousins, aunts, uncles, and grandparents. Huan agreed to go to Vietnam with her, for her, because he liked that she was so interested in his past. He never realized until afterward that her motivation to learn about Vietnam was to prove to her family that he really was Asian, not just black. Her work went unfinished. She broke up with him after realizing her mother would never ultimately approve. Maybe if he were half-white it would be different, all Asian even better. She offered to buy out her half of the trip. She even suggested he still go with someone else.

You know, we arranged reunion tours for the adoptees last year, Sophie says, looking at Huan. I thought we sent the information packet to you.

He feels the others' eyes on him, expecting an explanation for the rejection. I couldn't take off work, Huan says.

That's too bad. Sophie grins. You would have enjoyed it. We organized the adoptees to visit the orphanages or maternity hospitals where they were first found. If I remember your file correctly, you came to us from Blessed Haven. That's just south of here in the Delta.

We're going to the Delta, his mother says. Tomorrow as part of our tour.

How lovely, Sophie says. Well, if you'd like to visit, I could make a call.

That would be wonderful, Gwen says, eagerly leaning forward.

Huan doesn't bring it up until after they leave the center.

He wants to wait until they get back to their hotel room, but he can't. They are in a taxicab, Mai sitting in front, and Huan tries his best to keep his voice down.

I never said I wanted to visit the orphanage.

Gwen looks at him, surprised. Why wouldn't you?

Maybe I don't feel like it. Maybe today's been enough.

I don't understand, she says. Why would we come all this way without talking to the people who once knew you and took care of you? Sophie says there is a nun who believes she remembers you.

You don't get to make that decision for me.

Why are you getting so angry?

If I wanted to do this, I would have asked. The reason you asked is because you wanted to.

Fine. If you don't want to go, we don't have to go.

They're already expecting us.

I'll call Sophie tomorrow. I'll fix it, don't worry.

Gwen is crying. From the front seat, Mai reaches over and hands her a tissue. For the remainder of the ride, they listen to street noise from the driver's rolled-down window. In the sun's noon position, Huan can see the city's smog hovering over its inhabitants. They breathe the pollution in easily, accepting the foul sight and smell as natural.

In a dense forest forty-five miles outside of Ho Chi Minh City, a guide in faded green army attire leads the tour group to an open-sided hut. They sit in dusty plastic chairs while a woman in black pajamas turns on the big-screen television.

Beautiful shade trees and smiling, simple Vietnamese peasants, nature, serenity, safety in the town of Cu Chi. And then the looming American B-52s unleash their bombs. Bursts of gunfire crackle from the television speakers. Clouds of smoke overwhelm the screen, making the peasants on screen cry and suffer. Out of the dust, the valiant Communist liberators emerge. Young, beautiful, courageous faces. They will rescue their country.

The female guide must notice the audience fidgeting uncomfortably. She appears to expect this, laughs as she turns the video off, explaining that it is old, times have changed, and everyone, American and Vietnamese, are all friends now.

For their paying friends, Cu Chi Tunnels, the 250-kilometer underground headquarters of the Viet Cong during the war, is now a popular tourist attraction. The maze of tunnels especially widened to accommodate larger Western sightseers, a recreational firing range where visitors can shoot AK-47 rifles, souvenir booths selling Zippo lighters, pens made from bullets, rubber sandals, keepsake T-shirts.

Leah and the Vietnamese tunnel guide assure their group that the tunnels are safe and well maintained for the public. They are both much shorter than Huan.

The tunnel guide climbs down the ladder first, and one by one, each traveler follows. Some of the older, heavier people struggle to fit down the snug hole, with Leah's help. The ceiling in the underground areas barely reaches six feet and the tunnels themselves only three. They get on their hands and knees and crawl farther into the tunnels, the guide in front loudly reciting the tunnel's history.

Huan can't help admiring this vast underworld. These Vietnamese rat people whom the Americans so underestimated hand-dug and created a three-level network that once stretched to the Cambodian border. Protected by tiger pits, punji stake traps, and firing posts, the tunnels successfully endured American bombs, allowing their intricate subterranean maze to flourish with kitchens, hospitals, sleeping chambers, and even a small theater. The American veterans are especially impressed, their eyes memorizing these once mythical caverns, finally permitted to see Charlie's side.

The damp earthy walls and moist air are making Huan dizzy. He is tired of bumping into people's sweaty bodies, aware they can't help it, but desperately needing space. There is no space here. Everyone is on top of each other. These Cu Chi guerrillas must have had incredible endurance. Huan feels he is not selfish about many things, but air, he decides, he cannot share.

As they crawl into another narrow tunnel, Huan stops, falling back on his heels. Although the guide has advised them to take small, short breaths, he inhales a lungful of stale air and immediately begins coughing.

Hey, Mai says. He feels her hand on his shoulder. You okay?

The exit is only twenty yards ahead. Huan creeps faster. When he sees sunlight poking along the walls, an adrenaline boost propels him forward, fingers digging through the clay earth until he reaches the surface. Then he remembers Mai is behind him and helps pull her out.

At the next tunnel-crawling station, which the guide warns is even smaller and longer than the first, Huan decides to sit out. Mai offers to keep him company and he doesn't argue.

They sit at a rusted picnic table, next to a B-52 crater pit the size of a small fishing pond.

I'm not claustrophobic, Huan says.

Yeah, Mai says. Neither am I.

No really, Huan says. It was very unreasonable down there.

I agree.

Huan takes a long drink of the bottled water he bought at a

vendor's cart. The water tastes cloying, metallic, and Huan suspects it is a used bottle, refilled with tap water. A skinny boy carrying a pail of soft drinks sneaks up to them, tapping Huan on the shoulder. Coca? he asks, grinning and nodding vigorously.

Huan shakes his head and looks away. But the child is persistent. He runs to Huan's other side and asks again.

No buy, Huan says firmly.

It doesn't work. He won't leave, even when Mai sternly scolds him in Vietnamese. The boy pants loudly and steadily through his mouth. Whenever he feels Huan glancing his way, his posture straightens, his arms struggling to raise his scratched pail higher.

Help me, the boy says. Buy fresh Coca. Help me.

When the child nudges him again with the pail, Huan slams his water bottle down on the table, startling the boy and Mai.

I don't want your stupid drink, Huan says fiercely. Get the hell away from us.

The child jolts in shock, his mouth dropping open. Huan realizes the boy probably doesn't understand what he said, it is just the yelling that scares him. The boy's eyes turn red, his jaw begins to shake. But instead of tears, the child lets out a terrible howl.

You look down? the boy screams, dropping his pail. No better! You no better! The child is shaking violently, like he is suffering a seizure.

Mai stands up, trying to put a hand on the child's arm, but he ignores her, angry with her, too, continuing to scream. Tourists wander out of the gift booths, staring. The boy is crying in such terror. Finally, one of the tunnel guides rushes from the gate and grabs the boy by the arms, dragging him away, howling.

The boy's pail has fallen over in the rage, his soft drink cans scattered over the dusty ground. Mai begins picking them up.

I can't leave my hotel room, Huan says.

You didn't have to yell at him, Mai says, setting the pail on the table.

I know, Huan says. It was stupid.

Then why are you doing it?

I don't know. I don't know why I'm here.

You didn't want to come?

No. I was talked into it. I knew better, too, that's what pisses me off. Finding the past doesn't make anyone feel better when it's just bad.

What's bad?

Are you kidding? They hate me.

Who?

You've seen it. Cops, little boys, everybody.

Mai shakes her head. They don't even know you.

They don't have to. They hate Amerasians. They wish I didn't exist.

You can't blame them for not wanting to be here. They didn't do this.

I did?

Yes. Whoever said learning about your past is supposed to feel good? This is you, Huan, about how you feel. You're the one who hates them.

Huan sees two Vietnamese guides taking a cigarette break. They never wanted me, Huan says.

You don't know why your parents gave you up.

I'm supposed to accept that? It's different for you. You know your mother died and didn't abandon you on purpose. I have nothing to go on.

Do you really want answers? Then go to the orphanage tomorrow. I'll go with you.

It didn't help going to the adoption center.

That was your fault. Do you know how many orphans would love to know their histories? Remember Kim? She has no idea. And look what happened to her—married to a man she doesn't respect, with kids she doesn't want. You're taking it for granted.

Right, I should be more grateful.

Mai stands up suddenly. Forget it.

I'm sorry, Huan says. Really, I'm being a jerk. I don't mean to snap.

I know, Mai says, looking up. There's our group. We should go.

Across the woods, Huan can see the guide beginning to pull their travel companions from the hole in the ground. They poke their heads out and emerge into the sunlight, disoriented, panting for air. His mother is one of the last to surface. Her hair is disheveled, face pink with perspiration. She looks around frantically, until she sees Huan. Her relieved smile is genuine. Huan finishes his water and rejoins the group.

In the morning, they take a ferry and bus ride to the Delta, which, Leah says, is often referred to as the rice bowl of Vietnam. Out of the city, the air is fresh, the landscape clean and unspoiled. The tour charters a banana boat ride through local estuaries, where villages of wooden huts balance precariously on tall stilts and half-naked children splash in the yellow water. They visit a floating market and gaze at sampans overloaded with colorful vegetables, fruit, and fish.

Huan sits between Mai and his mother on the boat. While Gwen and the other tour members exclaim wonder over the various sights, Mai remains silent. Huan observes his friend, who seems absolutely unaffected by the scenery around her. In retrospect, Huan realizes that Mai hasn't really expressed any great pleasure or disappointment in their last few days of sightseeing. She has declared no favorite landmark. Except for food, she has purchased no souvenirs.

During the bus ride through the rice paddies, Huan's mother spots a peasant family plowing a field with a water buffalo. Though Huan pleads with her not to, his mother convinces Leah to stop the bus to take pictures. Some of the other tourists think it is a good idea, too, pulling out their own cameras. The peasants appear irritated, confused by all the attention. His mother squints behind her camera, fiddling with the zoom function, trying to capture the perfect photographs. When she reboards the bus, smiling with satisfaction, Huan can't even look at her.

For lunch, they feast on a home-cooked meal at a family's sugarcane plantation. The food is diverse and sumptuous, probably not what this albeit wealthy family has for lunch every day. Everything, the housemistress joyously boasts, is fresh from the Delta: catfish, mangoes, rice, cabbage, pork, poultry, and, of course, sugar.

The tour group is encouraged to spend time exploring the grounds of the plantation estate. Huan stands at the balcony, looking down at the winding rows of sugarcane. Huan's mother approaches him, tapping him on the shoulder hesitantly.

I talked to Sophie this morning, Gwen says. She said that they won't expect you, but if you change your mind, you are welcome.

Okay, Huan says.

So I think you should. I think you want to, and if my being there will be distracting, then I'll stay with the tour.

Huan considers this. You sure?

His mother blinks in surprise, and Huan realizes she really does want to come. Yes, she says. Of course.

I'll see you tonight, Huan says.

Huan finds Mai outside, silently watching the laborers shuck sugarcane. Do you want to go? he asks.

Mai looks at him in confusion, then remembers. Oh.

You don't have to, Huan says. The afternoon activities they would miss include visiting a snake farm, a silkworm factory, and a Buddhist pagoda. Maybe she'd rather do that.

No, Mai says. I'll go.

They make plans to meet up with the group that evening for the ferry ride back to Ho Chi Minh City. Huan's mother insists he take her camera, in case he might want to take pictures. Leah arranges for a motorbike taxi to take them to the orphanage, which is near the Vinh Long province.

They drive past Delta villages, where the poverty is even worse than the homeless they see in the city. Young girls slap wet clothes against large rocks in the river. Small children run after their taxi, fading in the clouds of dust the motorbike kicks up.

After following a long dirt road for nearly twenty minutes, the taxi driver slows. Unlike the adoption center, the orphanage doesn't appear to have been renovated since Huan left. Only half a gate remains as the entrance to a run-down building connected to a chapel. Vegetation stretches over the chipped concrete walls.

Inside, Mai talks with a younger nun, Sister Trieu, who takes them to the prayer room to wait for Sister Phuong. She is one of the few remaining nuns who worked at the orphanage when Huan was still there.

Mai sits in a wooden chair, waiting, while Huan paces around the room.

Where are the kids? Huan asks. It is too quiet. He can hear his own footsteps and breathing.

Maybe it's not an orphanage anymore, Mai says.

An older nun comes in with Sister Trieu. They converge in the middle of the room. The three women talk, and Huan listens. Occasionally, the older woman looks at him, but then returns to speaking with Mai.

Mai turns to Huan. Sister Phuong says she remembers you.

Huan nods and smiles obediently.

Sister Phuong points at Huan's face and laughs.

Mai smiles. She says you've grown into your big ears.

They confirm it is still an orphanage, but it is on the second floor. Sister Phuong invites them to come upstairs with her to look around.

In a small office stuffed with neglected bookshelves and filing cabinets, Sister Phuong peers over a large record book, fingering each name down the list, turning each page slowly. Mai and Huan sit across from her and wait. The office door is open, and Huan can hear the children moving around on the floor. They are remarkably quieter than the orphans at the adoption center, not much laughter or yelling, children's usual markers. Maybe it is naptime. One young girl passes their door. Her shoulders hunch over, her feet shuffle across the floor. She isn't curious enough to look in at the new visitors.

Ah, Sister Phuong says, looking up triumphantly. She gestures for Huan and Mai to come to her side and look.

The print is faded and nearly illegible. Huan looks at Mai.

It's your name, Mai says, her eyes lifting from the book. You weighed six pounds when you arrived. They estimated you were only a few days old.

Huan stares at where the nun's finger is still pointing, the first evidence of his existence. Though he realizes the information is sketchy and unreliable at best, he believes it.

They walk through the nursery, where Sister Phuong says Huan lived. It is a large room with rows and rows of wooden cribs. Several nuns tend to the crying children. Some of the babies are strong enough to stand, their small hands gripping the rails. Most, however, are not.

Sister Phuong asks if they'd like to hold a baby. It occurs to Huan that the older nun may think he and Mai are a couple, perhaps wanting to adopt. But Mai wants to. She holds a baby girl close to her chest, caressing the child's face and cooing into her ear.

What do you think the chances are of this baby getting adopted? Mai asks, looking at Huan.

I don't know.

Mai presses her lips against the child's forehead. The baby struggles in Mai's near-suffocating embrace. Yes, you do, she says. The Babylift is over.

The taxicab is supposed to pick them up at four o'clock, but it is late. Since Mai and Huan have already said their good-byes, they stand at the orphanage gate by the side of the road, waiting.

You know she really can't remember me, Huan says.

What do you mean?

You saw the book. There were a dozen more on the shelves. There were hundreds of babies. Do you really think she remembers one baby from over twenty-five years ago?

Mai glares at him. I think she was very nice.

I'm not saying she wasn't nice.

Why would she lie to you? What good does that do? You were here, you know they took care of you and found you a good home, and you still want more?

Why are you so upset?

You have so much to be grateful for. And all you've done since coming here is complain.

Okay, enough. Stop acting like you're so fine with everything here.

Excuse me?

I don't love it here. And neither do you. If you did, you wouldn't be living in China or Japan. We both have a right to be pissed. This country orphaned you, too.

Just because I'm not disowning this country every other minute doesn't mean I don't have problems with it.

I know, Huan says. He takes a breath. Then why don't you ever talk about them? Why can't you just tell me?

Mai shrugs, looking away. I don't know.

They sit on the dusty ground, leaning against the concrete wall, shoulder to shoulder.

I haven't said anything, Mai says, because I'm not sure.

Huan waits for several breaths until he speaks again. Why haven't you come to Vietnam until now? You must have had chances.

I always meant to. I think I got scared. I didn't want to go alone, or even when Gordon offered to come with me. When Gwen called, I knew this was my chance. She looks at Huan. I knew I could come here with you and your mom. Even if I wasn't completely ready yet.

Is it hard for you to be here? Huan says. At an orphanage?

She shakes her head.

Were you in an orphanage? Huan asks hesitantly. For all the years he's known Mai, she has never talked about this, beyond admitting a few facts. But now that she has seen so much of his past, he feels more comfortable asking about hers. He thinks she might want him to.

No, Mai says. She pauses for a long time.

My mother was from the North. No one knew who her family was when she died. So our neighbor used the money my mother left behind and some of her own to put me on a boat escaping from Saigon. She attached a note on me that I should be adopted by an American family. I still have it. The social worker gave it to me a few years ago.

Huan knows very little of the boat refugee experience except what he has read in textbooks. The escapes were difficult, horrifying even, especially if they were caught by the Communists, or worse, Thai pirates.

Do you remember the boat ride?

I remember sleeping a lot. They kept telling us kids to sleep so we wouldn't think about how hungry we were. We got sick. I don't even remember how we got to the refugee camp.

Do you remember your mother?

A little. I was very young. We used to sleep in the same bed. When she was still alive she used to comb my hair, which she let grow long because she thought it was pretty. When she died, our neighbor cut it off. It wasn't practical. I cried so much. I thought I looked like a boy.

You're lucky that you knew her.

Mai glances sideways at him, annoyed. Huan, you have a mother.

Huan pulls away from her. I know that.

Then why does it matter if your biological mother willingly gave you up or not? Why do you only care about the people who've rejected you?

I don't.

Your mother tries so hard. Mai shakes her head. It might feel suffocating sometimes, but all that effort—it's for you.

The taxi still has not arrived. Huan looks back at the dilapidated convent and orphanage, his first home. Can I ask you another favor? he says.

What?

Huan hands her his mother's camera. He jogs over to stand in front of the orphanage and waits for her to take the picture.

Huan can never really complain about his parents. They always showed him love, even during his angry years when he threw their devotion into their faces, sneering that they treated him like a charity case, their trendy Vietnamese baby whose life they rescued. How could they really love him? They didn't even know him.

They forgave him for all of this. They continued to love him, even when he couldn't believe or accept it. Though the workers at the orphanage and adoption center looked after hundreds of babies, Huan realizes they aren't to blame either.

It is Sunday night in Ho Chi Minh City, and the youths of the town are out to celebrate. They don their best clothes, buff their motorpeds to a shine, and prepare to coast the streets. There is no speeding or weaving through lanes tonight, no near accidents trying to rush from one place to another. No destination. The pleasure is in the journey, in the twenty-kilometer-per-hour ride.

It is Huan's idea to go out. It isn't on the itinerary. His mother is tired from their day in the Delta, but it is their last night in Ho Chi Minh City. Tomorrow they leave for central Vietnam. Huan hears from the hotel concierge that downtown on Sunday night is not to be missed. They are on vacation. Surprised but pleased, Gwen agrees to go out with him and Mai.

They sit at a sidewalk café on a busy boulevard, with an

unobstructed view of the cruisers loitering on the streets. Children effortlessly balance on the back of motorbikes without holding on, smiling and waving at passing friends and family. High school girls with bobbed black hair sail through traffic on bicycles, their brilliant white *ao dai* fluttering behind them. Street musicians strum mandolins and whistle into flutes for spare change. Teenage boys ignite firecrackers in the alleys, splashing smoky colors into the ink night.

I'm sorry you didn't come, Huan says to his mother. Mai has left to browse at the gift shop next door. That I didn't let you. It would have been nice.

I'm just glad you went. Gwen smiles at him. He thinks this isn't enough of an apology, but she is his mother. She knows who he is.

Mai returns with a gift bag. She shows them a deep red jade bracelet she has purchased. It is smooth, unblemished, with flecks of gold in it.

It's beautiful, Gwen says. It will look lovely against your skin.

It's for a friend, Mai says. But thank you.

Though it is getting late, the streets still grow crowded. They share the roads generously, so different from during the day when people viciously maneuver for room. For cruising, the more, the better. Huan's mother cannot resist any longer. She must come closer and take pictures.

I was afraid of hating everyone here, Mai says.

Huan looks at her.

They sent us to America because of you. Mai shrugs her shoulders. Our parents saw pictures of you full of food and in rich people's arms. They thought we'd get that, too. But we came too late. We weren't babies anymore, so nobody wanted us. It was no different from Vietnam.

Nearby, a little girl claps two blocks of wood together, enticing customers to come to her family's pho stall for fresh noodle soup. Eager patrons squat on plastic footstools, slurping warm broth, simmering beef strips, and vermicelli noodles.

How do you feel now? Huan asks.

I know better. It's not our parents' fault. Or anyone else's here. How could I be angry with them, expect them to do right when there was no such thing? When everything here was wrong?

Huan nods, understanding. It was a war.

It was.

They look out onto the street again. The cruisers, so proud and happy. They are young, born after the war. They only know Ho Chi Minh City, while Saigon is a memory that their parents and grandparents speak of. Their futures are pure.

A young man and woman slowly ride past the café. He is wearing a leather jacket, his hair slick with styling gel. She wears a bright yellow dress, her hair in a braid down her back. The woman's arms are wrapped around the man's waist, not because she needs to, but because they are obviously in love. When the couple passes their table, they wave. After a moment, Huan and Mai wave back.

ACKNOWLEDGMENTS

Special thanks to the following who helped make this book possible:

The University of Iowa Writers' Workshop, the Maytag Fellowship, and the Money for Women/Barbara Deming Memorial Fund, for their support during the writing of this book.

My fabulous agent, Dorian Karchmar, for her unflappable energy and wise insight. Alicia Brooks, for finding my book a home, Sally Kim, for her inspiration, George Witte, and everyone at St. Martin's Press.

Shirley Peck-Barnes, author of *The War Cradle,* and Cherie Clark, author of *After Sorrow Comes Joy,* for their nonfiction accounts of Operation Babylift.

My teachers, especially Lan Samantha Chang, David Wong Louie, and Chris Offutt.

Matt Shears, my first reader and best friend, who always pushed me to write the hardest scenes.

Most of all, to my parents, A.T. and Teresa Phan, whose wisdom and perseverance inspired me to put it on paper, and my brother, Andrew, for always believing I failed those premed classes on purpose so I could be a writer.